Addie's Sketchbook
Summer in Wellfleet

by Ruut DeMeo

The Omnibus Publishing
Baltimore

Summer in Wellfleet / Ruut DeMeo. -- 1st ed.
ISBN 978-1-7335985-8-3

Library of Congress Control Number - 2021937948

For permission requests, email the publisher, subject line:
"Attention Permissions Coordinator"
at
info@omnibuspub.com.

www.theomnibuspublishing.com

Book Design ©2021 The Omnibus Publishing
Cover Design by Jeff Chenault

Quantity sales. and special discounts are available on quantity purchases for promotions, fundraising, or educational use. For details, contact the "Special Sales Department" at info@omnibuspub.com.

To Sammy & Alice

and our Cape adventures

June 5th

Here we go again. Carmen gave me another sketchbook. It's tradition. I love traditions! Yes, please. I like knowing that every year, after we get in the car, I'll find this sketchbook waiting for me.

Mindy knows this about me. She reminds me all the time.

She's pretty swell for a bestie. Always noticing my good sides. Haha. But it's true. It would be really weird if Carmen and I didn't drive to Wellfleet on my birthday every year.

Okay, yes, last year was the ONE time we didn't (because of ART CAMP!), but we've had this tradition since I was two. How else would I know it's my birthday? I've always celebrated through tollbooths, vacation traffic, and at the New Jersey Turnpike's "lovely" rest stops.

So, I got what I always get for my birthday: a sketchbook. Mindy's getting an iPhone. Her birthday is in August. It's, you know, "for middle school." Carmen says she can't afford it, so I didn't even bother asking. I guess it would be nice. But whatevs.

Pop won't greet us at the door when we get there.

6

I wonder what it'll even be like NOT seeing him waving and grinning when we pull into that driveway. The worst part is that I didn't even get to see him last summer! And now I'll never get to see him again.

We didn't visit Pop last summer, because Carmen had to travel to Cambodia. She sent me to an ART CAMP for five weeks. (The camp was pretty awesome, though, and actually last summer's sketchbook probably has my BEST drawings ever).

Addie Kinsley ♡

I begged her to let me stay with Pop instead, but she said she didn't want to "burden him." Turns out, it would have been my last summer with him. He died in August.

Obviously Carmen didn't know he was gonna die. I think she still feels bad about it. Every now and then she does things to make up for it. Like today. Get this: we just stopped at a gas station somewhere in Connecticut and Carmen bought me a PURPLE DONUT from Dunkins. She NEVVVERRR usually buys me anything with food coloring.

Ahhh. It matched my hair.

It tasted like chemicals.

I loved it.

Three more hours to go on the drive... BORING. I'm gonna try to take a nap. Carmen just turned on NPR - it's the perfect thing to lull me to sleep. She thinks I'm listening to "This American Life," cause she keeps saying, "Hmm. Did you hear that? Some people have such incredible struggles." Haha. I just say, "Yep," and pretend I'm listening.

Carmen is all about the struggle! She's naturally drawn to people who are going through hard times. Like this one time, (and I know I said I was gonna take a nap, and I will as soon as I tell this story), this family down the street was having a yard sale and she went over there and bought tons of crap from them. I'm sure they were so relieved to get rid of their junk, but she was all, "They might be having a yard sale because they need the money! You never know, Ads!"

Come to think of it, whenever I ask her for money, she tells me: "Why don't you have a yard sale and sell some of your old books?" Not a chance. I am NEVER selling my books. Especially my comics, or anything that's even slightly illustrated.

Okay. Now I really am gonna take a nap.

TO BE CONTINUED...

9

We made it to 17 Old Wharf Road. Finally.

I was right. It was awful walking up to the cabin without Pop standing there! I just about cried, and I HATE crying. Everything is so different. The walkway was all overgrown with weeds - Pop woulda never let that happen. I mean, he was 72 but he still kept the garden so nice and neat. Dangit!! I really miss him. I don't know why, but it doesn't feel at all like his cottage anymore. The rooms don't smell all musty or like mothballs, the way they've always smelled whenever we got here on June 5th. And now I miss that horrible smell!

UMM.... WHOA...Carmen just called me into the kitchen after she'd opened her laptop.

She's like, "Ads! Get in here!"

GET READY.

WHATTTT???

WHY DIDN'T SHE TELL ME??? This summer was already gonna be bad without Pop. Now, it's gonna be **H-O-R-R-I-B-L-E.**

Doesn't she know that Mindy and I have all kinds of plans for surviving middle school TOGETHER??

We've even started our stockpile of safety gear:

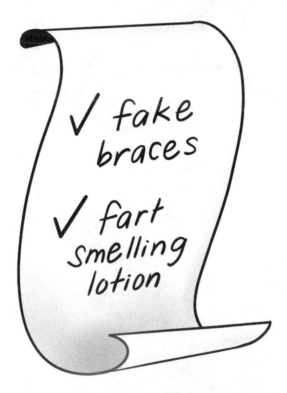

✓ fake braces

✓ fart smelling lotion

PLUS a collection of dorky quotes and off putting language. I mean, we probably would've been ignored anyway, but we've been PREPARING to be left alone. TOGETHER.

And now Carmen is telling me I have to GO TO ANOTHER SCHOOL? Without Mindy?

I'm SO mad at her!
The WORST part is that she sent my sketchbook from art camp last summer with the application, and THAT'S why they accepted me!

She was all like, "Ads, I thought you'd be happy!" and I just gaped at her open mouthed, because I couldn't think of anything to say. I am literally SPEECHLESS!

How could she do this to me???

June 6

I'm still SO mad at Carmen.

This morning, she made me coffee (COFFEE!? She's DEFINITELY trying to get on my good side!) and asked me to sit down.

WHAT? What does that have to do with anything? I told her it's because I've always called her Carmen. And she was like, "No, you called me mommy until you were three."

Well, OKAY. But for TEN years I've called her Carmen, and it would be really weird to start calling her mom all of a sudden.

Besides, the reason I started calling her Carmen is AWESOME. She told me I was obsessed with the words "car" and "mine" when I was three. And the best part is that her real name is actually Brigitte. HAHA! So, I gave her a way better name. Carmen suits her dark hair and loud laugh way better than BRIGITTE.

(Kinda how Addie suits ME better than Adeline, which is such a girly name. Ugh.)

Back to my ART SCHOOL DRAMA. It's just another dark cloud over my Cape Cod summer! I don't WANT TO GO to a different school! And it really hurts that she sent my sketchbook without asking me.

Now drawing has to be all "official" and stuff! I've always been able to just doodle as I please, and not really have to explain anything to anyone. What will it be like to have to draw on command?

I can just imagine it:

You know what? I'm just NOT gonna draw EVER AGAIN. Boom! See what you did, Carmen?

MORE LATER...

"Old bay chowda"

Yes. That IS a drawing.

Clearly I'm not gonna be able to keep my promise to never draw again.

Carmen made me her famous "wellfleet soup," which is basically chowder made with Old Bay seasoning.

EYE ROLL

Carmen is not exactly a top chef. But it tasted so good. It almost made me cry.

WHAT IS WRONG WITH ME?!

Tasting that soup brought back all the memories with Pop.

I'm so sad.

Also, it's supposed to rain for three days straight, and Carmen has a huge work thing that's due, so she's definitely not gonna drive me anywhere. UGH!!!

I just had a BRILLIANT IDEA.

I was going to start a bonfire in the backyard and use the sketchbook pages for kindling. But then I was, like, who am I kidding? HAHAHA.

INSTEAD...

I am gonna pretend that it's LAST summer and Pop is here. Yep. I'm gonna pretend I'm NOT at art camp, but I'm here, with him, doing all our favorite stuff!

RAIN!

Change of plans. I was gonna go fishing today and pretend Pop was telling me I was holding the rod all wrong. But now I'm stuck inside.

Actually, Pop and I used to play "spit" when it rained. He has this deck of old, fraying playing cards, where all the kings and queens look like they are at a luau.

I'm gonna go look for them.

Be right back...

OH MY GOD!!!

Just when I thought this summer could not be ANY WORSE, Carmen drops another BOMB on me!

I was looking around for those playing cards, and started noticing that, like, ALL of Pop's drawers and closets are EMPTY. I asked her, "Carmen, where are all of Pop's things?" And she just looked up from her laptop and said, "Oh, well, we rented the cabin out, so I had all his stuff put into storage."

And when I asked, "What do you mean WE RENTED THE CABIN OUT? Who's WE? And were the renters, like, people we DON'T KNOW!?" She was just, like, "Yeah, Addie. How do you think we were able to pay the mortgage and taxes for it? This is Massachusetts. Taxes are super high here."

When I asked "who's we?" again, she said she had to get back to work.

This is CRAZY!

I'm gonna try to doodle, even though it suddenly feels SO WEIRD to be in this room.

STILL MAD.

Mad... and SAD! I miss Pop SO much. Wish I'd had a chance to say goodbye. I miss the way he ate a muffin. He pushed the loose crumbs together with his fingertips. And the way he used the plastic bags from the store, over and over, until they could barely hold anything.

I looked through all the closets and drawers a second time, for anything. Like, even one of his bandannas. He used to wear a wet bandanna when he worked in the garden to stay cool on a hot day.

It's kind of a brilliant trick... I've tried it ↘

I used to think his bandannas were so gnarly. I mean they were all faded and stained and stuff. And here I am now, digging through drawers, crawling under beds, looking for even a piece of one. Why did Carmen have to put EVERYTHING in storage?

I can't stop thinking about how there were actually other people living here. It's weird! And it wouldn't be so bad if they hadn't left behind a bunch of their things!

Here's what I DID find:

⭐ stuffed koala plush in linen closet

⭐ US puzzle in bottom drawer in my room (Texas & South Dakota are missing)

⭐ Weird foreign book in coffee table drawer

⭐ Half-used toothpaste & ugly pink nailpolish

Maybe they're planning to come back in the fall? Or maybe they're just slobs. Or super forgetful. That stuffed koala is legit, though. I've seen that kind at Five Below. They're like, five bucks a pop.

(HAHA! Of course they are, it's FIVE BELOW.)

If I left a toy like that behind, I would make my mom turn the car around and come back for it. Yeah. It's true. I love all my stuffies like family members, which is why I leave them at home, in their designated places. Who am I kidding? I've also named each one, with middle and last names, too. And I've given them birthdays and made them social security numbers.

ANYWAY...

Carmen told me to leave the renters' stuff alone, but I think I'm gonna have to take the plush koala and the puzzle to the thrift shop at the back of the church. It's just WAY too depressing for me. (The book I might keep, though - you know how it is with ME AND BOOKS. It looks like Russian, maybe? I'll google translate it later, when Carmen falls asleep on the couch with her glass of red wine. Lol).

LOVE all the detail!

But the illustrations are WAY COOL. I'm gonna do a quick sketch of my favorite one.

(It's kind of t-r-i-p-p-y!)

while I was drawing that owl, a car pulled into the driveway across the way. It's a Subaru, and it's so red, that it made me instantly crave that candy apple I had at the fall fair.

Never told Carmen about it. All that Red #40! Mindy's dad even asked me if I wanted another one, then bought me a funnel cake, though I DID ALMOST ask for another candy apple - just cause I could. Mindy got a caramel apple and then had toffee stuck in her braces all night. Even when she sang on stage! It was FUNNY!!!

So, anyway. I jumped off my bed and spied on the candy apple red Subaru, and waited to see who would get out of the car. My heart was kinda beating fast, cause I thought MAYBE it would be Miller!!! (And maybe his family got a new car?) I haven't seen Miller in two years.

But it wasn't Miller. Or his family. I won't lie: I was hoping it was him. I don't have a crush on him or anything. He's just kind of crazy. He makes me laugh. Or at least he used to. We used to ride our bikes down to the inlet and dig for clams. We sneaked around the old graveyard. But of course, this IS officially the worst summer ever. So why do I think I'd get to have a friend? (And anyway, how do I know if Miller hasn't turned into a total jerk? Pretty much every boy I know is a jerk. Why wouldn't he be one too?)

No idea who that guy is. I mean, he's black, so he's probably not Miller's family, plus I've never seen him before. (Maybe Miller's family is renting out their cottage too?) I didn't see the Subaru Guy's face, he had a hood over his head. He only brought in one bag of groceries out of the car. Excuse my Sherlock Holmesiness, but we just got here yesterday, and this is the first I'm seeing this guy.

BUT THEN... Drumroll please...

He came back to the car and opened the back door and VOILA! A little pug jumped out! O.M.G. That pug is the CUTEST. It was wearing a RAINCOAT! It ran around the car, all frantic, and then it SNEEZED a bunch of times in the rain. I was laughing so loud that Carmen heard me in the kitchen. She was like, "Ads, you losing your mind in there?" Haha.

YEAH CARMEN! I am losing my mind! The rain is never going to stop!

And now I'll have way less time to doodle, because now I have a full-time job of SPYING ON A PUG!

P.S. I google translated a page in that kids book. It's in POLISH. DUH! (Turns out Russian is like, not the same letters as English AT ALL. Haha).

Here's what the text said:
przyfrunela ptasia policja I tak sie skonczyla ta lesna audycja

WHOA!

Here's the translation:

"The bird police flew over and so this forest broadcast ended."

Google is so dumb. No kids book author would ever write that. Even in Poland. I also googled "candy apple red" and "pugs" and "Texas" and "South Dakota." I was bored.

June 8

Rain update: it's raining.

I think that red Subaru-guy takes his pug on more walks than any other dog owner in history. Maybe he's trying to reach 10,000 steps every day, and has somehow outsmarted his Fitbit to include the extra little pug steps. (Hahahaha!) Or maybe it's a new dog and so he's introducing every street to the dog, like, "This here's old wharf road, and this here's schoolhouse road," etc. But no. Not that guy.

I can't put my finger on it, but I find him weird. He just walks kind of jerky and always has a scowl on his face. Sometimes I swear he looks right at me, even though I'm hiding behind the curtain.

More developments. I've basically stayed inside for 3 DAYS now, except earlier today, Carmen drove into town and I hopped in the car with her. I don't really want to hang out with her, but, like, what else is there to do?

We found out the church doesn't take donations on Tuesdays, but only on Fridays from 1-1:30. HAHA. Old church people are pretty funny. They're all, "my schedule is PACKED with old people aerobics and walking real slow to the mini mart! This is the only time I've got available to pick up donations from vacationers!"

Well, I hope my schedule is clear then, because that is, like, a really small window for me to make my big koala plush toy donation! I'm actually kind of worried that I'll get all attached to that darn koala by then.

Shoot. Then I'll have to baptize it with a full name, give it a birth certificate, a social security card, and, like, give it a backstory. And I guess it will have to be a Polish name, since I'm pretty sure the people who rented Pop's cabin were Polish.

The other thing we did in town was stop in at the bookstore to see Carmen's second cousin, Philip.

YAY!!! LOVE THAT STORE!

He was just closing, so we didn't actually get to stay very long. BUT... And this is a BIG BUT, and the first *GOOD* thing that has happened since we got here:

DRUMROLL...Philip asked if I wanted to stop by tomorrow and HELP him. I mean. Work. At. The. Book. Shop.

WHAT?!

I know. Most people would be, like, "whoop-de-doo. Shelving used books. Boring." But I am not most people, and I actually can't imagine anything more fun than unboxing and sniffing, touching, (sneak-reading), organizing and sliding books into shelves ALL DAY LONG.

So... Yeah. And it's weird, cause I always just assumed that Philip hated me. He's always been kind of a jerk. But then he, like, shocked me big time by saying, "Hey, Addie, do you want a little summer job? I could pay you ten bucks a day?" I had to consciously restrain myself from gawking.

Carmen was annoyingly excited for me. She freaked the whole six-minute car ride home, saying over and over, "That is so nice of him. Isn't it so nice of him? You're gonna have so much fun."

über to drive-in
Movie ticket
Hamburger
Fries
milkshake
$50.⁰⁰?

I really wanted to freak out too, but I just kept checking out my purple hair in the side view mirror and I practiced all of my socially awkward faces. (I'm getting really good - Mindy would be proud of me).

I can make at least FIFTY BUCKS a week!

And you know what? I don't care if I have to go to the movies alone. Who needs friends? Maybe I can ask the Subaru-guy to let me take his pug? And the whole way I can just narrate for the pug, like a tour guide:

"This here is Route 6A, and that there is Wellfleet's oldest cemetery and that's the road you take down to the beach."

Maybe the pug won't care about Cape Cod geography. But then again, maybe it will seal our friendship forever.

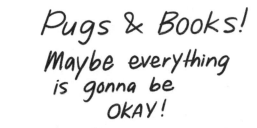

Pugs & Books!
Maybe everything is gonna be OKAY!

I love the bookstore. Why? Because it has *BOOKS* in it. I only brought a couple graphic novels to the Cape with me, because I knew I'd be getting more from Philip's store. The best part is not finding out what he has in stock. It's a used book shop, so mostly it's vintage books. And stuff I've never heard of.

June 9

STILL RAINING.

I'm going NUTS. I can't keep sitting around this empty house anymore! Carmen's been staring at her laptop all day - she says she just HAS to meet this deadline for some proposal. I know it's a grant for a non-profit "that helps underserved populations." Whatever. I'm the only population she needs to care about right now.

I mean, I'm her KID! And it would be nice to be driven to the beach, or to get ice cream, or to the bumper cars, or the drive-in theatre.

LATER...

I'm a the bookstore. I rode my bike here. Philip is having his lunch in the back, while I man the counter. No one's come in since I got here.

Here's what happened:

I got so bored at the cabin, I walked up to Carmen and asked her about my dad. Honestly, I just did it because it always gets her to look up from her laptop. It's like magic. Boom. Works every time. She looked up, and just blinked at me over her glasses and said, "I've told you. You're better off without him."

And then, because I was extra mad, I said, "What about Kyle? I've only met my big brother ONCE. You know, he's seventeen now, which means he probably has a license and a cool car. He could drive me around. And we could do fun, cool stuff together." She didn't say anything, but I could tell what she was thinking by the look on her face:

Even if Kyle came here you and I both know he'd stare at an Xbox and not drive you around!

Okay, maybe I don't know what Carmen was actually thinking. Maybe that's what I was thinking. But then she started screaming at me.

"Don't you see I'm under a bit of stress here? Who do you think has been paying our mortgage all these years? You

35

think Steve's child support check put even a dent in it? I don't want you to ask me about either of them again, okay? I'm trying to make a living here, so, please, Adeline, just stop pestering me about your dad!"

I said, "Okayyyyy, geesh..." and walked away. But inside I felt like a boiling kettle of some bright green explosive liquid. I went in the shed and FOUND MY BIKE! (Thank you POP! At least those renters didn't know to look in the shed.)

Nice and rusty!

Just the way I left it 2 summers ago!

I blew up the tires, then went back and put this sketchbook and some random other stuff into my backpack, threw on my rain jacket, and TOOK OFF!

It felt good to ride my bike. I didn't even care that my jeans were getting soaked. I rode all the way down to the wharf, past the boat yard and all the way through town. I ended up here at the bookshop, and Philip let me stay. Carmen hasn't called him. She probably hasn't even noticed that I left. She's such a nice lady, she's so dedicated to the underserved.

Well, I'm dedicated to these underserved books, and after Philip's done eating, I'm gonna help him unpack some boxes and shelf new arrivals. I'm pretty darn excited to see what all is in there. I gotta say, I'm awful happy I got this lil' job! It's nice just to have something else to do besides feel depressed about Pop, and never seeing Mindy again, and the fact that Polish people lived in Pop's cottage.

June 10

I was right! Carmen hadn't even noticed I was gone. I came home, she looked up from her laptop, and said, "Hey. You hungry?" She'd already poured herself a glass of wine, so I knew we would probably have leftovers. I was hungry, though. So I didn't care.

Anyway, yesterday was INTERESTING.

I ended up staying at the bookstore for a few hours. I helped put away three whole boxes of books that he'd just brought from Boston. There were some real gems in there. I was already eyeing a few Classics Illustrated comics, but then he had me write the prices with a pencil. $48 for the Sherlock Holmes one alone! I guess they are collector's items. FIGURES!

But yesterday, I had NO time to read. I had to shuffle around a bunch of titles without losing track of where they were supposed to be. At one point I got nervous, because I'd pulled out a handful of books from the poetry shelf, and forgot where I put them. I could tell Philip was getting annoyed with me, so I laser-focused and. . . BOOM! There they were, next to a pile of dumb self-help books.

Phew. Glad I didn't get fired on my first day.

But then... GET THIS. Subaru Guy came into the store! My heart was pounding. (Honestly, I don't know why.) He bought a bunch of paperback thrillers. THRILLERS! See? I knew there was something iffy about him! I could hear his pug barking in the car, and watched him from behind a shelf. He didn't even really look at the titles. He just pulled out four random ones, walked up to Philip, and paid with cash. Philip asked if he was on the mailing list, but he was like, "Mm. No, thanks."

Weird, right?

I have GOT to get to the bottom of this. Who is he? Why is he in Miller's house?

Today, the rain isn't so bad. I'm gonna go work in the store for a bit, and then do some investigating. Not sure exactly what that will be yet... Maybe I'll ask Philip what books he bought, and go from there. Watch out, mister! You have no idea how crazy this purple-haired girl across the street can be!

Haha... At least I amuse myself.

Philip didn't write down the titles that Subaru Guy bought. Shoot! And he got super annoyed with me, because I dripped rainwater all over the sale bin by the door when I came in.

work was pretty boring, I hate to admit. Probably because he had me rearrange the cookbooks. Meh. Although I did see this one interesting title:

I put it on the bottom shelf in case I have time to check it out later. Any crazy nut who took the time to write that book is okay by me!

The whole time I was there, only six people came in, and most of them were vacationers that I didn't recognize.

But then this older lady came in who looked familiar. At first I couldn't remember where I'd seen her. She had long silver hair, glasses with thick rims, and denim overalls. She browsed the art books for like ten minutes but didn't buy anything. Then, right as she was leaving, it hit me! I'd seen her once with Pop!

I ran after her and before she got into her truck, I said, "Excuse me! Do you remember Charles Kinsley?"

She turned around and said, "Yes. Of course I do."

We talked about Pop for a little bit. She told me all kinds of things, really fast. I'll try to remember everything...

1. She was sorry that he'd died
2. She told me he was usually at church on Sundays, and she always looked for him.
4. She said they weren't "sweethearts" or anything. Just friends.
5. Apparently he used to go over her place on Lieutenant Island for coffee and strawberry-rhubarb pie, and they would discuss different things, the weather, the water.

Love it! Pop had a NICE FRIEND!

> It was nice to have a friend who'd lived in Wellfleet as long as I have.

> He helped me out back in the shed quite a bit...

Then, she told me something kinda weird

That's why it was strange he wasn't at church.

Didn't you go by his house at all to find out why?

Yes I did... But there was a car in the driveway that I didn't recognize.

I got a weird feeling and almost didn't ask her. But then I did. I asked her what kind of car, and she said, "Bright red."

WHAT!?

And of course Philip came out at that EXACT moment and told me to get back inside. But she squeezed my hand and said, "Come by anytime. I'd love to sit and talk and remember your grandfather."

UMM... OKAY!!!

June 11

No time to write or doodle! A LOT happened today!

June 12

WHOA.

This is going to take me a WHILE. But I have to write down every detail. I didn't work yesterday. And it didn't RAIN! It was kind of overcast. (If Pop was still alive, he DEFINITELY would have taken me fishing. He'd have told me it was just the kind of day the fish would bite.)

Anyway, before Carmen woke up, I hopped on my bike and rode all the way out to see that lady — her name is Elaine — on Lieutenant Island. It took me a WHILE to ride there, and when I found her house, she didn't come to the door. I went out back and in her backyard there were all these really cool contraptions. This is what one of them looked like:.

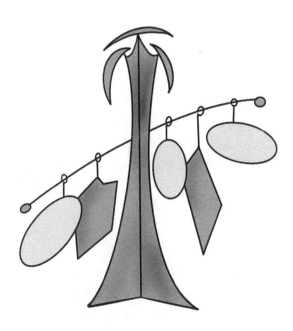

when she came around the corner with a shield over her head, I shrieked. She looked like a MARTIAN.

It was hilarious. And she is SO RAD! She showed me all her metal scraps in the shed. She welds them and puts them back together to make sculptures! I was very impressed. She's pretty cool for a little old lady!

Also, Elaine DOES make THE BEST strawberry-rhubarb pie I've tasted. I can totally see why Elaine and Pop were friends. (Duh! That was his favorite kind of pie!) It was so nice to talk about Pop with someone... She also noticed different things he did, like the funny way he would slurp his coffee. At times I felt a little jealous of Elaine, because not only did she get to hang out with him more, but she got to see him in the fall and winter and spring too. She knew all the stuff he did when we weren't here! SUPAH JELLY!

So, I finally asked her about the red car. I was like, "Are you sure it was parked in Pop's driveway, and not across the road?" And she nodded and told me she'd stayed and spied for a little while, (LOVE HER), and that she'd seen a tall black guy, a woman, and a little kid in the house. Annnddd.... DRUMROLL.... A LITTLE DOG! I asked if it was a pug, to which she answered, "I'm not sure." So, I showed her my recent pug drawings and she was like, "Wow, those are very good!" and I was like, "Focus, lady! Is this the kind of dog you saw?" then she was like, "Yes, I think so."

OMG, right?!

So, then I asked, "When exactly was this?" She had to think for a minute. "It must have been in early August. I hadn't seen Charles all summer. Not since June. And so, I went over to his house—"

"Didn't you guys ever just call each other?"

"No, we didn't. We were old-fashioned like that. I never even had his telephone number. And I don't have one of those mobile telephones. I suspect he didn't either."

(HAHAHAHA. I love old people!)

Pop refused to get a cell phone. He was real stubborn about it.

When I asked her about the last time she'd seen him, she said, "I ran into him at the wharf. I think it was the beginning of June. I'd gone to buy some fish, as I always do on Mondays. And there was Charles, all dressed

OLD PEOPLE! No PHONES ALLOWED!

in a suit, like he was about to go work in an office. He was shaking hands with some young chap who looked like a rich sailor, if you ask me. The man had on some of those pink pants they like to wear in Nantucket. It looked like they were in the middle of making a deal or something. I waited until they were done, then walked up to Charles, and said Hello."

I gaped at her. I was on the edge of my lawn chair. "And?"

"Charles said Hello back, he was very cordial, but seemed kind of nervous. On edge. He didn't tell me then what was happening. He didn't ask me what I was doing either, like he normally would have. I didn't pry about his suit or anything. We're from another generation, Charles and I. We don't discuss private matters, you know?"

(UGHHHHH. I hate old people!)

I kept asking her to think back. Did she see anything else? Did he say anything else? NOTHING. And all summer she didn't hear from Pop - the same summer I didn't come here. And she'd gone by his house in August, and the Subaru Guy and his family were there?

Elaine sent me home before high tide. Apparently, you do NOT want to get stuck on Lieutenant Island during high tide. The water rises around the road and covers the bridge, so no one can get on and off the island. (Sucks for anyone who might have, like, an emergency?)

It's Sunday today. Carmen just asked if I want to get a donut and go watch the seals at Marconi Beach. I'm still mad at her. But I LOOOOOOVE Marconi Beach. And I LOVE DONUTS! So, I'm gonna go. And who knows, maybe she'll tell me what REALLY happened last summer.

Official Declaration:

Carmen is the worst person on the planet. Or at least in Cape Cod!

We did pick up donuts and go down to the beach. The beach was SO beautiful! It was so nice to be down there finally, breathing in that salty air! It brought back all my favorite memories. I was feeling all mushy! I told myself I can forgive and forget everything. Like how she didn't let me come visit Pop last summer, and how she mailed my sketchbook to that art school without asking me.

I even told myself I don't care that she didn't let me grow up with my stepbrother, Kyle, that yeah, maybe he is a spoiled brat. And maybe my dad really IS a bad person, and that I'm better off without him.

There's something about the beach... It's magical. It made me feel like maybe everything would be okay after all!

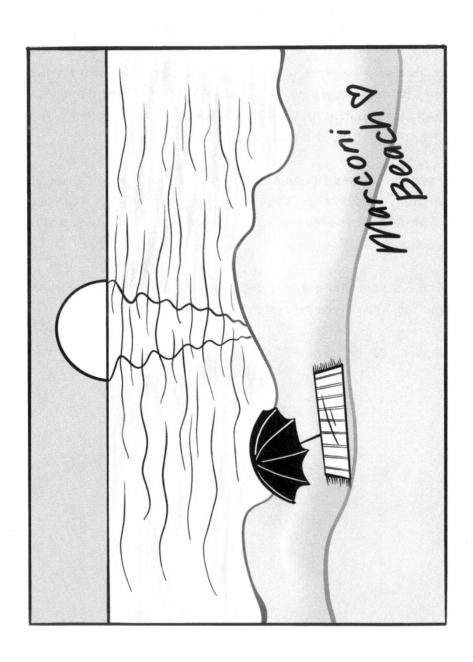

But then, I asked her about the Subaru Guy in the house across the street.

"Subaru guy?" She pretended not to know. But then it occurred to me that maybe she really HADN'T looked out the window the ENTIRE week. That was totally possible. So, I explained.

"There's a guy staying in Miller's house, and he has a pug, and a red Subaru. And this lady I saw at the book shop — her name's Elaine — told me she'd seen the same guy at Pop's in September—"

"You spoke with Elaine?" Carmen cut me off. "When?"

She was getting all hung up on Elaine, so I said, "I asked you about Subaru Guy. Do you know him?" I felt like such a real detective, not letting my informant distract me with their shenanigans. But she is my mom, so she somehow managed to take over the investigation, and soon — I don't even know HOW it happened — I was being GROUNDED for sneaking around all over Wellfleet, being nosy, and for "hanging our private laundry out to dry in public."

WHAT??

How do moms do that? How do they take YOUR top secret agenda and turn it around so that YOU — the Sherlock Holmes character — become the person of intrigue, possibly even the CRIMINAL? I am literally being punished for doing NOTHING except making friends with a sweet old lady, and asking about a mysterious guy who lives in Miller's house, and has possibly even stayed in ours. Who is he? Some kind of serial Air BnB'er, who's on a mission to stay in every house in Wellfleet?

But most importantly, how can Carmen GROUND ME during my summer vacation?

Let's face it — THAT IS THE REAL CRIME HERE.

Name: Carmen Kinsley

Age: 34

Crime: grounding daughter on vacation.

June 13

Turns out, Carmen isn't letting me work at the book shop either. Maybe she HAS paid attention to me at least a little, because she knows it's like the WORST punishment to not let me be around BOOKS. She locked my bike in the tool shed. Ha. Like that's gonna do anything.

"How long do I have to stay here?" I asked her, pretending I hadn't already packed my backpack with random stuff I might need if I decided to escape.

"Your summer vacation will start when you decide to stop interrogating me about your Pop, and about your Dad, and everyone else." She looked like she was about to cry, and for a minute, I actually thought about putting all my stuff back. Her face made me feel guilty that I'd planned on running away.

"Ads, listen," she finally said, "when I heard that Pop had died last year, I just about lost my mind. You probably think I'm some cold-hearted witch because I rented out his cabin. But it was too hard to have to come here right away—"

"I thought you said we needed the money."

"Well, yes. I had to make a financial decision too. But it was also an emotional decision. I was mourning him. I'm still mourning him. And it's just easier if we don't dig up the past, all right?"

"But..." And I hesitated, knowing that if I asked her more questions, she might do something crazy, like sell the TV, or make me take a bus back to Maryland. But I couldn't help myself. "Elaine told me that Subaru Guy and his family were here in August. How can that be? Wasn't Pop here when he died?"

"What did I just say?" she cut me off and started freaking out. (I should have kept my mouth shut.) "Didn't I JUST tell you to stop asking about him? Addie, you have to believe me. You are better off not knowing certain things!"

I'm better off NOT KNOWING things?? Like about my own sketchbooks being mailed to an art school behind my back? Or what it's like to grow up with a DAD? A BROTHER? How am I better off not knowing what happened to my grandfather?

Doesn't she know me AT ALL? Telling me not to ask about something is basically a DARE to find out about it on my own!

June 14

Well, I was about to start my investigation. But something came up. GET THIS:

DRUMROLL...

I Am Dog Sitting!

Here's how it happened: I was taking out the trash when Subaru Guy walked out of the house. The pug saw me and ran right up to me and OH, MY! I ALREADY LOVED HER!

At first, Subaru Guy didn't say anything, he just stood there and let me play with the dog. Then, he asked me a question.

And I KNEW:

"Didn't I see you at the book shop?" he asked, with a VERY BRITISH accent.

(What's going on? The European invasion of Wellfleet?!)

"Yes," I said. "But I'm grounded right now."

"Grounded? As in, being punished for something?"

OH MY. His accent is LOVELY!

"Yes, that's what grounded means. Don't kids get grounded wherever you're from?"

"Well, I'm from Boston. So, I imagine yes." He stuck his hand out. "Raymond. And you must be Adeline?"

"Uh, yeah. Nice to meet you."

That pug was licking me and being all silly. It kind of snorts when it breathes and OOOHHHHH I just love HER! Then, the CRAZIEST thing happened. GET THIS:

"Listen," he said and knelt down beside me (he is actually nice! CRAZY, right?) "I have to drive back home to Boston this afternoon, just for a day or two. How would you like to take care of Iris while I'm gone? She doesn't do all that well inside of moving objects. She's the reason I'm here, instead of sailing." He made a pretend throw-up face and stuck out his tongue. It was HILARIOUS!

"I'd have to ask my mom, but I'm sure it would be fine!" (I had no idea what Carmen would say, but actually, I didn't care!)

"That would be fantastic. Iris might do better here at my house, so I'll just leave the cottage unlocked for you."

This was the moment of truth. It was HARD, but I had to ask him.

"So, this is your house? Do you know Miller, the boy who used to come here?"

"Of course I do. He's my nephew. And, yes, this cottage belongs to me too."

"Oh, so, are you his mom's brother or something?"

"No, I'm married to his... It's complicated."

"I don't mind. I'd really like to know. Please tell me."

I probably sounded REAALLLY desparate!!

But let's face it— I AM!

I need to know what's GOING ON!

"I'll tell you what," he said. "You take good care of Iris and we'll have a chat when I get back. Does that sound all right?"

Basically, EVERYTHING that Raymond says aloud sounds ALL RIGHT! He sounds like a character from a *Harry Potter* movie! It's FANTASTIC!!!

"I should ask Carmen first."

"It's all right with me." It was Carmen. She was standing in the doorway. "Hey, Raymond. Good to see you again."

"Hello, Brigitte. How are you?"

"I'm all right," Carmen said. "Still a bit sad, I guess. But glad to still have this place."

Then Raymond said to me, "Looks like your mum says it's all right with her. And I promise we'll have a chat when I return. I'll even bring your favorite pop from the grocer. What's your flavor?"

ANNDDDD THAT IS WHAT A-C-T-U-A-L-L-Y HAPPENED.

Now, Iris is sitting at the foot of the couch, licking my toes. I'm completely obsessed with this pug! I can't even believe my luck! I get to hang out with her! While GROUNDED! She is SOOOO SWEET and FUNNY and CUTE!!!

First of all, she is a toe-licking machine!

She LOVES being warm, even if she's already panting, she HAS to crawl underneath a blanket!

She falls asleep on her back ALL THE TIME! It's hard not to laugh and wake her up... She kind of jerks her head up to see who dares to disturb her, but then she plops back down and falls asleep again! It's ADORABLE!

I thought about sneaking around in here to find out more about Miller's family... But honestly, drawing pictures of Iris is WAY more fun! Besides, Raymond promised to tell me when he gets back.

I guess it's ALL RIGHT not to be working at the bookshop right now! But only because I've got IRIS!!!

June 15 — the day of DOOM

THIS IS BAD

I can hardly breathe Iris is missing!

We can't find her anywhere. Please, god, pleeeeeaaaseeeee!

It's all my fault!

This is the WORST SUMMER O.M.G.

IRIS!!!! where is she?????

Raymond came back at around eight o'clock, only to find his dog MISSING. It was HORRIBLE! I will never forget the look on his face.

I told him I was with her ALL day. We played and played, then took a long walk and she was so tired. I left her sleeping in the house and came home at around six, to eat my dinner real quick. When he got home, she was NOWHERE! He said the back door was cracked open. I must have not closed it properly — I'm SUCH AN IDIOT!!!

Raymond and Carmen went to look for her in their cars. I'm sitting here on the front stoop, in case I hear or see her. But I can't just sit around anymore. I have to do something! I NEED MY BIKE! But Carmen has the key to the shed.

I ran around the neighborhood calling for Iris for a while.

Carmen came back at 9. She offered Raymond some wine but he just went home without saying much. He told me it wasn't my fault. He thinks she might have gotten confused about where Iris was, that she's not used to being out in the countryside.

(Actually, that DOES sound exactly like Iris. She is like a little old lady in a tiny dog body)

OH GOD! I could just DIE! I could tell that Raymond was so worried. And it's MY FAULT. I should have NEVER taken my eyes off her!!!

After we said good night to Raymond, Carmen sat down and opened her laptop. "We have to figure something out. Ads, come here. Let's figure this out together. You're good with Google and stuff."

I wanted to pretend I had no idea what she was talking about. But this was not the time. I took over and googled "how to find a lost dog on vacation" then "when a pug runs away" and "how do pugs do in nature?" then I searched for "Wellfleet neighborhood associations."

Carmen was watching me. "See?" she said, "I wouldn't have thought of any of that." And I just kept searching. It was like the tenth time today that I wanted to cry.

"This isn't helping," I told her. "Nobody ever checks these message boards. Look at this one. The last thread is from 2011. We just have to keep looking for her outside. We have to knock on everyone's door—"

Carmen hugged me all of a sudden. She said, "It's okay, Addie. I know you feel really bad about what happened. But maybe we should get some sleep now? We'll look for Iris first thing tomorrow, okay?"

And then I did cry a little. I'd expected Carmen to be really mad at me. But even with her arms around me, I just couldn't feel better. I was mad at myself, and as much as I wanted to be comforted by a mom (like a normal kid would), I just couldn't get over it.

After a while, Carmen fell asleep on the couch. I stayed up past midnight. I couldn't sleep, I just kept looking up stuff online, and all of a sudden I stumbled on this weird online news article about Wellfleet.

Wellfleet News

○ AUGUST 2017 ○

Man's Suit found in Tide Waters Under Lieutenant Island Bridge

It was from last summer. And my heart just about stopped. There was a picture of the tidewater flooding the bridge to Lieutenant Island. And I remembered Elaine telling me that she'd seen Pop in a SUIT...

And I couldn't help wondering if...

Could it be???

Carmen told me Pop had died of some kind of cancer. But, like, Pop was in really good shape. He was like a *young* grandpa, if you know what I mean.

what if she's hiding something from me about his death?

June 16

No sign of Iris.
Life is HORRIBLE. This is officially the WORST summer EVER!!!

I can't even draw. SEE???

June 18

when I got up yesterday, it was raining again. My first thought:

Carmen helped out for a while. We drove around. But then she had to keep working on her proposal. She's trying to get a government grant for a health project in Asia somewhere.

I know there are poor people there who need help and medical attention and stuff. But it would've been nice if she could've kept looking for IRIS with me!

When Carmen wasn't looking, I stole her keys, went out back and took my bike out of the shed.

IN MY BACKPACK:
* stuffed koala
* Polish book
* Sketchbook
* Bag of treats from Raymonds'

All day I rode around calling for Iris. I walked along the shores and sneaked around in people's backyards. One lady saw me and I told her what I was doing. She started calling for Iris too. It was kind of sweet.

I stopped by the bookshop and told Philip what happened. It was so warm and dry in there. I wanted to stay. But I was restless. I had to keep looking for Iris. Philip pointed at me and said, "You're dripping all over my sale books again. When are you coming back to work? There's a bunch more books I need you unbox."

And I was like, NO IDEA WHATSOEVER. This whole summer has blown up in my face. And IRIS IS OUT THERE, wandering around the Cape by her itty bitty self. She could be ANYWHERE! I kept thinking about the sixty bucks he owed me, and then he just handed me a TWENTY and said he'd pay me the rest if I came back next week.

STINGY PHILIP!

I was so desperate, I started riding toward Lieutenant Island... I was going back to Elaine's, even though I wasn't supposed to talk to her anymore. It was raining hard, and by the time I reached the crossing, water was covering the road. It freaked me out. I couldn't go to Elaine's after all.

I was starving. And mad. And I felt like crying, A LOT. I turned around and just kept riding and riding and ended up on Route 6, even though it was already getting dark. But would Carmen even notice I was gone? PROB. NOT.

I crossed over to the graveyard. (Miller and I went there two summers ago. We thought we were total DELINQUENTS. Hahaha. We looked at all the old graves and made up stories about the people.)

One thing's for sure: going to the graveyard wasn't NEARLY as fun without Miller. I mean, honestly, it was kinda scary, and it was getting dark. I was starving, so I sat down by a tree.

And then...

YUP. That was a first. It tasted like nuts and bacon and chicken. I was so hungry, I ended up eating the whole bag. I'M SORRY IRIS!!! The next thing I knew, I heard some guy's voice, "you all right, little fella?" It was morning!

I SLEPT IN A CEMETERY.

(Just when I thought eating the dog treats had been the low point! HA!) And the first thing that ran through my mind was NOT "Oh no! Carmen must be SO worried about me!" Nope. A normal kid with a normal family might think that. But ME? what did I do? I asked the man — who looked very creepy, if I'm honest — if he was a local.

"yes, I'm a local. why?"

RIGHT?? why DID I ask him that? But I didn't stop there. I was on a roll.

"Did you ever hear of anyone drowning under the Lieutenant Island bridge? An older man, specifically?"

He looked at me kinda funny and said, "You sure you're all right? Is there anyone you'd like me to call?" But he REALLY didn't look like the kind of guy who had a cellphone. I mean, he offered me a ride in his pickup truck, and that thing looked A-N-C-I-E-N-T. It was like that rusty one with gapped teeth from Cars.

BUT SERIOUSLY... Something is DEFINITELY wrong with me, because if there's anything I hate, it is surprises and stuff. Being unsure of things. And finding myself in unforeseen situations with strange people who I don't know. Yet there I was, conversing with a complete stranger about Pop! The only possible explanation I can think of for my sudden change of personality is:

From the minute we got here... Carmen telling me about the art school... about the renters... then her and Raymond KNOWING each other... and then me losing Iris... and Elaine's weird stories about Pop... I don't know. I might have also been delirious with hunger, or, like, poisoned from the dog treats, but when the guy offered to throw my bike in the back of his truck and give me a ride, I was like... "Okay. Sure."

WHAT THE HECK IS WRONG WITH ME?!

LATER...

Did I tell Chuck to give me a ride me home, like a normal kid (with a normal family) might do? Nope.

I accepted his offer to have breakfast! HA!

STAY
away
from strangers,
Addie!

But I was SO hungry and he said to order whatever I wanted. So I had eggs and home fries. They were super greasy and SO delicious! I even had some coffee, and now my feet won't stop doing a jig under the table.

JIGGLY FEET

Of all the years I've spent on the Cape, I've never even SEEN this breakfast place. It's kind of secluded...Can't see it from Route 6. But I paid close attention when we were driving. I know how to get home.

There are hardly any people here. And Chuck just left me here. He was like, "I gotta go do some things but I can come check on you later." And I said, "No, thanks. I can find my way." I watched him take the bike out of the back of his rusty truck and leave it in front of the restaurant.

Okay. So far so good. At least I didn't get abducted. I didn't tell him my real name or where I live either.

I don't really know what my plan is. I still have my twenty bucks.

OOOHHHH!!!! I have Carmen's keys!!!! WHOA!!!

Okay. This is both good and bad.

BAD: because Carmen will KILL me when she finds out
GOOD: because she is stuck at the cottage, and can't come after me (unless Raymond drives her). Also GOOD because, DRUMROLL...

There's a key on the chain that says Sun Self Storage, with the number H-69 on it.

We don't have a storage unit in Maryland. So it HAS TO BE POP'S STUFF! And it HAS to be here! At the Cape!

Okay. I'm gonna ride to a gas station and find out where Sun Self Storage is. Then I'm gonna look through his stuff! But first, I'm gonna look for Iris some more!

For the first time, I have a good feeling! It could just be the greasy home fries. But who cares. Right now, I really think everything is gonna work out!

LATER...

I'm sitting at White Crest beach. It's SO beautiful. Today actually turned out to be a nice beach day. In a perfect world, I would have a mom and a dad (and maybe a brother), and we would all be here together, like all the other families that are setting up their umbrellas and chairs. Iris would be safe at home with Raymond. (And Philip would stop being stingy.) In that "perfect world," I would also be going to middle school with Mindy this fall.

If I could just find Iris, that would be enough! But the world is very much NOT perfect. I looked for her, but didn't dare go back home. Not yet. I couldn't ride too close to our street, in case Carmen or Raymond, or any of our neighbors might see me. I'm not ready to face them yet.

Then, I rode up to that Sun Self Storage. It was about a 15 minute ride North. But I couldn't get into the compound. You have to have some kind of code to open the gate! I tried 69, and a bunch of other numbers, but nothing worked.

Now I'm starving again.

If I go home, Carmen will DEFINITELY ground me again. I can forget about the code. She'll never give it to me. And I can't face Raymond. Not only did I lose his dog, but I took off like a guilty criminal.

Continued...

I'd forgotten that I had that Polish book in my bag. Seriously, Addie! Way to pack a getaway bag.

Here's what
I should've brought:
* Food
* Water
* a change of clothes
* Cash
* an iPhone (I WISH!)
* a flashlight
* probably a knife or something for self-defense

And here's what I ACTUALLY packed (like an idiot): dog treats (already eaten), koala stuffy, bathing suit, Polish book, sketchbook and pens. HAHAHAHA

What would Pop say?

He would probably be, like, "Addie, back in my day we didn't have any of those fancy mobile telephones. We used maps and compasses to find our way."

Anyway, I looked through the Polish book again. I hadn't noticed before, but there's a name and a phone number written inside the front cover.

Anya Krakowski. 617 999 0880

I could call the number if I had a phone. How did people make phone calls before there were iPhones? SERIOUSLY.

Well, I'm officially not me anymore. I'm in Orleans, sitting on church lawn, waiting for 4 o'clock. I'm about to meet the lady who rented Pop's cabin!

HERE IS HOW IT WENT DOWN:

I walked up to a nice lady in the beach parking lot to ask if I could use her phone. I lied to her, saying I'd been waiting for my dad, and that maybe he'd gone to a different beach. She had two kids buzzing around her, but she looked concerned, so she let me use it. I dialed the phone number I found in the book.

"Hello?"

"Is this Anya?"

"Yes. Who is this?"

"My name is Addie. I found your book at a cottage in Wellfleet. It's my grandfather's house."

"What book you found?" (Kinda love her accent too!)

"It's a kids' book, I think. It has a picture of an owl on the cover—"

"Ohhhhh!!!" Then she said something in Polish and laughed.

"That belong to my daughter. I'm sorry. I didn't know we left it behind."

"So, it was you who rented the house?"

"Yes, we was there... From about September last year. Until some weeks ago. We found another place."

"Are you still in Cape Cod?"

"Yes. We're in Orleans now."

Orleans... I remembered going there a bunch of times... It couldn't be too far, so I did something CRAZY. (But seriously. Nothing I do shocks me anymore. I don't even know WHO I AM.)

"I could come there and bring you the book?"

"Oh, that's okay. I come by and get it. Maybe next week?"

"I really don't mind. I don't have anything else to do."

"You have a car? I'm sorry, but you sound like you're very young."

"I can get there. What time would be good?"

"I think we'll be back at four?" She spoke Polish again to someone.

Then the lady with the kids needed her phone back. She was scowling at me, like she knew I'd lied to her. Luckily, Anya gave me her address. I memorized it and handed the phone back. The lady grabbed it and caught up to her two kids, who were running down the dune to the beach.

Before, I probably would have been jealous of that lady's kids, she'd packed a huge cooler for them and brought a ton of stuff for the beach.

But I was on a mission.

I rode back to the gas station and bought a map (for $4.99! Shoot. Twenty bucks is really not that much money. Stingy Philip!) I found out there was a bike trail that went straight from Wellfleet to Orleans. WOOHOO!

So....

That trail was WAY longer than it looked on paper. It took me TWO AND A HALF HOURS to get here! But anyway. I'm here, and at 4 o'clock, I'm gonna knock on her door and ask her about last year... Maybe she'll know something about Pop!

P.S. I'm still deciding if I'm gonna give the koala stuffy back too. I've kind of grown attached to it. Luckily, I haven't named it yet... (I didn't have a chance to google Polish names! LOL)

June 19

I spent the night at Anya's. She is SUPER NICE! She made me dinner and everything. And now, I am absolutely POSITIVE that Carmen is hiding something from me about Pop's death. But first, let me start at the beginning…

I found the address she gave me — it's like an apartment in the back of a house. Anya answered the door. She's much younger than I thought. Her daughter, Sabina, came to the door too. She is adorable — she's five. I handed her the book, AND THE KOALA, right away. The kid was OVERJOYED!!! I was so glad I hadn't donated any of their stuff! I didn't say anything about the puzzle because I already knew I'd want to have a reason to come back here.

Anya made a yummy dinner: potatoes and sausage. I ate so much. It tasted SO GOOD. And while Sabina played with her stuffed animals (in Polish - CUTE!), Anya told me about what it was like to live at Pop's.

"I found advertisement online for cottage. I thought it was good price. I have a job in Wellfleet, housekeeping, and the cottage was close to my job. I called the number, I make check for Greg Sanders. Then, a guy met me at the house and let me in."

"Greg Sanders?"

Miller's Last Name is SANDERS! & I'm pretty sure his Uncle's name is Greg!

"Was it Greg who met you at the house?"

"No. It was Raymond. Black guy. Het us in and show us place. I gave him money, and every month, I mail it to Greg Sanders in Boston."

OK. So, that confirms what Elaine saw! But what the heck? Why did she pay Raymond to live in Pop's cabin?

Anya and I talked a little bit more after that. She made me some yummy tea — but I didn't get any more information about Pop. She didn't know anything about him, actually. Greg or Raymond hadn't told her anything. She just assumed the house belonged to THEM. It really weirded me out.

This morning, Anya said she could drive me home when she drops off her daughter and goes to work. I thought about offering to babysit, just so I could stay longer. But then I changed my mind. Let's face it, I am like the ABSOLUTE WORST candidate for watching anything smaller than me. Humans. Dogs. Fill in the blank.

I told her I'll ride my bike back. We'll see if I actually do. I might just bomb around the Cape today. I'm not ready to go home yet... But I DO want to get that code for the storage unit. How do I get it without Carmen knowing??

The thing is, if I go home now, Carmen will lock me in the shed. She'll "have my hide," as they say. But maybe I have to just face my archnemesis! LOL! Seriously, though... If she doesn't realize this is ALL her fault, then maybe I need to enlighten her. After being on my own the last couple of days, I'm starting to feel like maybe I don't need a normal family after all! Who needs a mom? Who needs a dad?? I can be on my own. I mean, I'll still live with Carmen, but I'll just wait 'til I'm sixteen or seventeen or whatever, and I'll save up my money. And then... BOOM! I'm OUTTA THERE. I'll go travel the world. Or... like, at least the DMV area.

"DMV" =
District of Columbia & Maryland
& Virginia AREA

Learned it
at a gas station
LAST WEEK!

I just figured out what to do next. I know someone who will help me.

MY SUMMER IN A NUTSHELL!

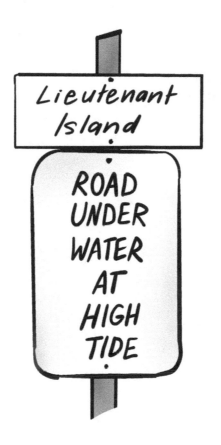

I rode my bike back to Wellfleet, all the way to Lieutenant Island. It took almost FOUR HOURS! I was STARVING and EXHAUSTED to say the least. Actually, I was D-Y-I-N-G!!!

When I got to Elaine's, she wasn't here, but luckily her door was open, so I sneaked in and drank a BUNCH of water. Almost threw up. But in, like, five minutes, I was fine, and I ate some toast and OJ and fruit. YUM! If any mom ever has a hard time getting their kid to eat fruit, they should just starve them for a day and make them ride across an island on their bike. YUP. Did it for me. I LOVE FRUIT NOW. I had an orange and an apple and a banana. And like thirty grapes. At least.

91

Elaine didn't come back for HOURS. I sat on her back porch doodling. It was such a nice day! CAPE COD SUMMER at its FINEST! I wandered around her property and found this cool little birdbath in the woods. Elaine is pretty swell, for an old lady and all. I mean, I think she should DEFINITELY get a cellphone. But other than that, she IS kind of EDGY with all her metalwork and stuff. I mean, she knows how to WELD!

I had fallen asleep in a lawn chair. She woke me up.

"HERE you are!" I could hear it in her voice. She'd been out LOOKING FOR ME? "I was just at your Pop's, helping your mother. She's worried sick about you!"

"Please don't call her. Not yet. I want to ask you something—"

"Well, I have to at least let her know that you're here."
I thought about Carmen worrying about me... I felt pretty guilty.

"She called the police, Addie."

"Oh." Suddenly I didn't feel guilty anymore. I felt SICK to my stomach. If I'd feared being a criminal before (for, you know, stealing Carmen's keys, and sleeping in a graveyard), NOW I felt like a FUGITIVE.

But Elaine must have seen how worried I was, cause she said, "Listen. I'll make you dinner and we can talk. You'll need to spend the night here anyway, because of high tide. But I have to call her first and tell her you're here. That way she can stop worrying about you. All right?"

It sounded like a pretty good deal, actually. At the rate this summer is going, I was most assuredly gonna end up in Juvie.

"Thanks, Elaine. I wanted to ask you about that bridge—"

"Hold on. Let me go call her."

I waited outside. I thought about Pop's suit floating in the water. Was it Pop's suit?

When Elaine came back, she had a serious expression on her face. "What?" I said. "What did she say?"

"It's about that dog."

"Iris? Oh my god! What happened?"

"They found her."

I jumped up and down like a total idiot. Then I stopped.

"Is she… alive?"

"Don't think anyone's forgotten about your little excursion, just because that dog was found. I'm sure your mother still has a severe punishment in mind for you."

"Okay, but… Is Iris okay?" Elaine stared at me a long time, as if she was deciding whether or not to tell me. It was TORTURE. The suspense was KILLING me! "Please, Elaine. Just tell me. Is Iris OKAY???"

Here is my BEST PUG DRAWING EVERRR

It's a MIRACLE! IRIS IS ALIVE!

Iris went on a little excursion too! HAHA. And she was SUPER hungry too - just like me! I wish I'd been there... I just KNEW that Iris and I are kindred souls. We were both "found" at the same exact time. The best part is that she'd gone wandering around, and then found her own way back.

It is a M-I-R-A-C-L-E!

HONESTLY. This is pretty much the first thing that's gone RIGHT this whole summer! (And maybe now, Carmen won't be as mad at me??)

I was A LOT happier after that. Elaine made me a veggie burger (it was OKAY...), and then she redeemed herself by giving me some more of that DYNAMITE strawberry-rhubarb pie. We stayed up late, talking and listening to music.

She didn't know anything about that suit found in the water, but she did tell me a bunch of stories about Pop. I begged her to keep going, even though it was totally making me cry. I might have been teary-eyed because I was so tired, or maybe they were happy tears for Iris.

But when she showed me the flower boxes Pop had made for her, I just couldn't hold back. I burst out crying, cause I remembered how he used to always have a project going. He'd have all his tools lined up on the workbench, and he'd be wearing that old bandanna. Apparently it was too much for me. I cried for a WHILE.

But Elaine just hugged me. Then she said that when we lose someone we love, putting on a brave face is a human mechanism for survival. (SHE IS WICKED SMART.) She said that maybe my mom has had to do that a lot, and I was like, "Nooooo….. Carmen doesn't do that. She's like a wreck. She cries all the time. For no reason."

And Elaine said, "But think about it. She's a single mom. She's raised you all by herself. Your Pop told me about how proud he was of his little girl."

This was news to me. I'd never actually thought of Carmen as his kid, to be honest. I asked Elaine to tell me EVERYTHING Pop had ever said about Carmen. It wasn't much. But it was enough to get me wondering again.

"Your Pop didn't talk about her that much," Elaine said, "but what little he did tell me, I could sense that their relationship was complicated. He'd be proud of her one minute, then the next he'd say, 'I hope she knows what she's doing, traveling to all those foreign countries.'"

I asked Elaine to explain it to me, because it's never even CROSSED my mind that traveling to foreign countries is a problem. She said, "Well, I've told you this before: I think Charles was very old-fashioned. He worked hard all his life. He loved his routine and hadn't done much traveling. I honestly think he simply didn't have a need to leave Massachusetts. He liked a simple life. He even used to curse about all the rich people who built mansions around here, saying they were ruining the landscape. I agreed with him. We always said there was a reason why Cape Cod houses were built so small, hidden below the tree tops. It was so that Cape Cod would always look the same. It's not like that anymore, unfortunately."

I know she's right. Pop never even visited us in Maryland. I could see why he might have been mad at his daughter for traveling, especially in June. It meant a break in the routine. I'll bet he hated it so much that he got sick.

I mean, I almost died when Carmen told me she'd mailed my sketchbooks to that school. Some of us are just NOT meant to handle change!

Hanging out here at Elaine's makes me wish I'd lived with Pop instead. He was the only normal family I ever had. He worked all year, then spent his summers here in Wellfleet. He fished. He cooked the fish. He went to church. I'm starting to dread going home... I don't want to live with Carmen anymore. I don't want to go to that stupid school.

I need a PLAN.

June 20

I didn't go home right away. I wandered around Wellfleet.

I went to the beach and watched the early morning walkers come down with their dogs. I watched the waiters serve coffee to lazy hotel guests at the resort. Then I spied on Philip as he got out of his car and opened the bookstore.

I rode around town, watching other shops open up. I just saw the mail truck come through. Tourists are all lined up for breakfast at the one little restaurant.

I've been thinking about Pop the whole time, about how much he must have loved spending his summers here in this small town. I'm a little depressed, to be honest, thinking about everything that's happened. Even the thought of Iris doesn't cheer me up.

I will go home today. After this. But only to tell Carmen what I've decided. There's something she has kept from me, and I'm not gonna let her do that anymore.

WHOA!!!!!!!!

I was gonna ask her to open up the storage unit. HAHAHA... I was mistaken to think I could ASK HER for anything!

It all happened SO FAST. RE-CAP:

I rode home. My stomach was ALL in knots — I was SO nervous to see Carmen. But then I saw another car in the driveway, next to ours. At first, I didn't recognize it. But as soon as I walked in, before I turned into the kitchen, I KNEW, and I heard his voice.

"Ads?"

Carmen heard me come in. She didn't run to me and hug me, like a normal mom would. She just stood there, leaning against the stove, sipping her coffee. And of all people, my estranged FATHER was sitting at the table. He looked like he'd driven there straight from a construction site.

"Hey, Steve. Why are you here?"

"See?" Carmen said to him, TOTALLY ignoring me. "She doesn't even call me mom. Maybe that's something you can work on together."

"What do you mean?" I asked.

"You owe your mother an apology." Steve said.

"What?"

"You heard me. Apologize to her. She's been worried sick about you. I came this morning to make sure you never do anything like this again. What the hell's the matter with you anyway?"

I was IN SHOCK. "What do you mean, to make sure? What are you gonna do?"

"Apologize first. Then we'll talk."

I looked at Carmen. It was hard, but I finally said, "I'm sorry."

"Sorry for what, Ads? For losing the dog? For going behind my back and taking my keys? Or for contacting our renters? Yeah. I know about that, too. Do you even know how unprofessional that is? But how would you know that? You are thirteen! You live in your own dreamworld. You think you can just do whatever you want! But I have news for you, okay? You can't. You're a kid. And you know what? You don't deserve to have that bike. I'm keeping it here—"

"Bridge, calm down. Let me talk to her."

Carmen was SO flustered, but, like, he somehow managed to get her to calm down. It was impressive.

"It's true," Steve started. "You need to own up, Adeline. Now is your chance to make things right with your mother. Or else you'll have to come stay with us for the rest of the summer."

Then something weird happened. Carmen put her coffee down and crossed her arms. "I thought we already agreed," she said to Steve. "You're making it sound like she can stay as long as she apologizes to me. But I told you I need you to take her. I thought you understood that. I mean, isn't that why you drove all the way out here?"

"You're sending me away? To live with... him?"

She looked at me.

"I just lost three days of my life to worrying about you. I was completely freaking out. Do you think I was able to get a single minute of work done? My boss is having a cow. How do you think there's food in the fridge? And gas in the car?" She stuck her hand out. "Give me my keys, right now."

And then she kept going.

"You think money just appears in my bank account? You need to start respecting the fact that I am the one who feeds you and clothes you. You need a lesson. And that is why you're going to stay with your dad for the rest of the summer."

"But what about my job?" Steve tried. He obviously wasn't ready to take me with him.

I felt like a load of dried up cow dung being kicked around.

"She's gonna have to be at the house by herself."

"What about Kyle?" Carmen asked. "Can't Kyle watch Addie?"

"I'm not gonna mess up his summer—"

"I don't care. Mess it up. It's your turn. I'm done worrying about Addie every minute of every day."

I was so shocked I couldn't even think. I just stood there, feeling my eyes get all tingly. I dug in my backpack for the keys and kept telling myself...

AND that is how my life turned to absolute RUBBISH!

I didn't even get a chance to see Iris. He gave me, like, six whole minutes to pack my things. I cried, seeing the blue IKEA sheets on my bed that we'd brought for the summer. WHY WAS THIS HAPPENING TO ME? I wanted more time. I wanted a chance to explain. I had so many more questions.

The drive here took two hours. Steve lives just outside Boston. I'm sleeping in his spare room on a futon. It smells like dirty socks in here. He has to go to work tomorrow, and told me there is NOWHERE to run, as if I'm some CRIMINAL.

Kyle is not here, and when I asked about him, Steve just said he's out with his friends.

"Does he have a car?"

"Yeah. But he doesn't have to drive you around, if that's what you're getting at."

"Why does everyone hate me?"

"Oh, stop it, Adeline. Nobody hates you." Steve looked at me weird. It almost looked like HE was gonna cry. He started to explain stuff to me, even though I definitely had NOT asked him to.

He said, "I was surprised to hear from your mom yesterday. I've tried to come see you guys at the Cape over the years. She's never let me come by. I surprised you once when you were little, though. You must've been turning five—"

"Yeah, I know. Why do you think I'm still scared to death of clowns?"

Steve laughed. "I thought it would be funny to surprise you in a clown mask. After that, though, she told me not to come. So, I've stayed away. But you should know that at least I tried. I wanted to be part of your life."

"Well, you are now. Thanks to the worst summer ever."

"The worst summer? Why?"

I considered telling him. But seriously, would Steve actually understand?? Did he REALLY care? If he knew me at all, he would have known that even at age five, I HATED surprises. Steve is literally the reason I can NEVER go to a circus. I just said, "I miss Pop. That's all."

"I see." Then Steve pulled out the cereal and milk and left for work.

I knew he wouldn't understand.

It's weird to think that just a week ago, I had a job at a BOOKSHOP, and then I was DOG-SITTING the most adorable little pup in the world... I had a BIKE... And now, I am STUCK in an apartment outside Boston with NOTHING.

HEY!!! I just remembered something!

I think MILLER LIVES IN THIS TOWN!

June 22

Kyle came home. I guess HE'S allowed to come and go as he pleases! I can't help but wonder what it would've been like to be raised by Steve instead of Carmen. WELL, if she used to think he was a terrible dad, she doesn't seem to care anymore! She just sent me to live at his house. LOL

Anyway... Back to Kyle, the brother I've only met ONE other time. He just walked past me into his room. I tried to act cool, like I didn't care that he was even there. I stood behind his door for a while. I could barely make out the sound of him talking on the phone. His video game was SO LOUD.

Then he popped out of the room all of a sudden. I almost had a heart attack!

After a few minutes, I knocked.

"WHAT?!" Kyle still didn't turn off the music. I could hear he was still on the phone. Giggling, kind of like he was talking to a girl, maybe?

"I need to find a friend of mine," I said, as loud as I could. "He lives nearby. I just need help finding his number."

Kyle paused the game and told the girl he'd call her back. When he stepped out, I got a peek at his room — he is SPOILED! — he has, like, a computer AND a TV and an Xbox. And I was, like, why didn't I grow up with Steve instead??

I followed Kyle into the kitchen. He got himself a coke out of the fridge and said, "Steve warned me about you."

"Yeah?" I said. Then I realized Kyle had just called him Steve, instead of dad. "Did Steve tell you why I'm here?"

"You think you're so hard core. Running away with your bike?" He laughed at me and almost spat out his coke. "I mean. It's kinda cool I guess."

"Oh. Thanks. I only did it cause I was trying to find out what happened to my grandfather. And there's this kid in town who might know something. I'm pretty sure his uncle rented out our cabin. It's kinda weird. " Kyle was scrolling on his phone, chugging his coke. "So... Do you think you could help me find him? Could we look, like, on Facebook or something?"

"Facebook?" Kyle laughed. "Nobody's on Facebook anymore." Then he shocked me and asked, "what's the dude's name?"

"Miller Sanders. And I know that about Facebook. Duh." I was in absolute DORK MODE. OMG. Mindy would have kicked me SO HARD.

"This the guy?" Kyle showed me a picture. I nodded. Miller looked like himself, posing with his skateboard. But somehow older. Even cooler. "He's on Insta. You have a crush on him or something?"

"No. I told you. His uncle... whatever. Can you, like, send him a message?"

Kyle exhaled like he was already exasperated with me. "And what do I get for helping you out, Sherlock? Got any money?" I pulled out the fourteen and change I'd kept in my pocket. I dropped a quarter on the floor, like a nervous idiot.

"Nice," Kyle said. "This'll get me some cigs." He laughed. "You get an allowance or something?"

"No, I had a job in Wellfleet."

"Ooh. A job." He burped, then reached into the fridge for another coke and grabbed a bag of chips out of the cupboard.

"What'd you do? Dog-walking?"

"I worked in a bookstore."

"Makes total sense."

"What's that supposed to mean?" I sounded more defensive than I'd intended.

"Um, it makes sense because your mom is, like, a total nerd. No idea how your mom and my dad ended up together. Let alone made a kid. I mean, Steve's pretty much never cracked open a book."

"Oh... well..." I wanted to ask Kyle what else he knew about Carmen and Steve. Where did they meet? How did they end up together? But instead I tried to act cool and just said, "That explains a lot about Steve."

"Okay, so, you want me to hit up this boy, Miller, and then what? Like, drive you to the mall, so you guys can make out at Hot Topic, or something?"

WOW. I couldn't believe $14 and change got me ALL THAT.

"Yeah, that would be awesome. Except for the making out part. We're just friends."

"Not a chance." Kyle took his snacks, went back in his room, and turned his game up even louder than before.

WHAT A JERK!! AND he took my MONEY!!

I almost thought I was gonna see Miller! That would have been AWESOME... So much for that... **DANGIT!!**

June 24

There is NOTHING to do here. Also, Steve is the WORST cook. He offered to give me five bucks a day if I do the laundry and vacuum and stuff. At least I've made my $15 back.

Tonight, some woman came over and brought pizza. Her name's Christy. It's SO WEIRD that Steve has a girlfriend. I mean, it's not like Steve even feels like my dad, so I shouldn't care. But still. It's just WEIRD. Too many changes at once.

At least Christy's kinda nice. She's sleeping over here. She said tomorrow we should go to a lake together. I'm actually KIND OF EXCITED that we're, like, going on an excursion as a "family." Hahaha.

Steve let me borrow his phone. I called MINDY! It was SO GOOD to talk to her... I almost CRIED. What is WRONG WITH ME?? She's having the BEST summer. Totally unfair. She's been at the beach. EVERY. FREAKING. DAY.

I started telling her about how it's been the worst summer ever... But then I stopped and just talked about Iris for a bit. I mean, I don't want to RUIN HER SUMMER, too. But I did ask her if she could find Miller on Instagram. She said she'd try to sneak on her mom's phone later. GOOD OL' MINDY.

Saturday night

WHOA!!! Today was T-E-R-R-I-B-L-E. But I'll start at the beginning again. We went to this lake called Highland. Christy had packed sandwiches (like a REAL mom! HA) and it was sunny out, and even Kyle came and didn't act like a total butthead, so I was hopeful that we'd have a good time. But he stared at his phone pretty much the whole time, except when he fell asleep in the sun (and got a sunburn, HA-HA!)

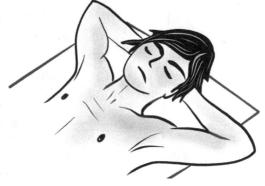

ANYWAY...

After lunch, I saw this kid walking toward me. I thought my eyes were LYING to me, because it looked JUST like Miller.

Mindy had messaged him through her mom's Insta! He showed me the message:

I should be grateful to Mindy... That WAS pretty sweet of her! But now I'm wishing that Miller had NEVER come to see me at the lake.

First of all, it was slightly awkward because he's, like, a LEGIT teenager and has a low voice and everything, and I am SO underdeveloped. I was already feeling kinda insecure and my boobs probably shrunk even more from the shock of seeing him.

But then, for like a whole hour, he was just Miller. We actually had FUN. We didn't swim or anything, we just walked around and talked and had ice cream.

I told him how weird it had been in Wellfleet without him or Pop. I told him everything, why I'd been sent to live at Steve's, about working at the bookshop, and dog-sitting for Raymond, and sleeping at the graveyard—

"You SLEPT at the graveyard? Our graveyard? Dude..."

"I know. And then this weird serial killer looking guy picked me up in a truck that was literally covered in rust."

"Picked you up? As in, you went with him?"

"Ya. I have no idea what's happening to me. I'm like a totally different person all of a sudden. I'm not dead from the shock of living with my dad and stepbrother. These are people I've only met, like, once or twice in my whole life."

Miller stared at me for a long time, then said, "Nah. You're still the same Addie."

And that's when I realized that Miller is probably my oldest friend. I've known him for way longer than Mindy. "You know, it sucked being in Wellfleet without Pop. But I think I would've been okay if you'd been there."

He shrugged. "We haven't gone for a couple years. I don't really know why. We might go in August. Greg and Raymond say to go anytime. I mean, it's not like they're hogging the place or anything. There's plenty of room—"

"Greg and Raymond?" A lightbulb flicked on. "Are they... Is he...?"

"Married? Yeah."

"Ohhhhhh." I slapped my forehead. "That's why he said it's complicated."

"Not really. They've been together for, like, twenty years. I've never seen my Uncle Greg with anyone besides Raymond. They met when they were teenagers. They met on the Cape, actually. I think your mom was friends with them. Didn't she tell you?"

"No." I felt uncomfortable being interrogated, so I had to go into detective mode. "So, actually, I wanted to ask you about something. I went to see this lady, Anya, and she told me she paid your Uncle when she rented out Pop's cabin. Do you know anything about that?"

Miller did that awkward chewing his cheek thing, like he was hiding something from me. "No," he said, and just shrugged.

I elbowed him and said, "Come on. Your uncle takes money from someone who's living in our house? That's super weird. I know you know something."

He stopped walking and let out a huge exhale. "All right. I didn't want to tell you."

My heart started pounding. "Tell me what?"

"Well. I think your Pop was, like, in really bad trouble."

"What do you mean? With the law or something?"

He chuckled. "No. I think he couldn't pay for the house. I don't know the details."

"That's ridiculous. Pop owned the house."

Miller just shrugged. "Like I said, I don't know exactly what happened. All I know is that Uncle Greg had to basically, like, give him a bunch of money. To bail him out."

My throat felt really tight all of a sudden. I could barely breathe. It was SO awkward, and NOT AT ALL what I'd expected.

"This is so stupid. I'm sorry that Mindy messaged you."

"Addie, it's fine. It's good to see you—"

"Yeah, except you just made my summer like a hundred times worse. I can't believe you said that about Pop."

Then Miller got really unpleasant all of a sudden. "Just because he was your grandfather doesn't mean he was perfect."

"I know that! But he was perfect to me, okay? And I don't want anyone telling me otherwise. Especially you."

"Wow."

"What do you mean, Wow?" I was getting really irritated.

"I don't know. It's just kinda immature of you to think he was perfect. He was just a person, you know? It's, like, better to face the truth about people. I think."

"I do know the truth about Pop. He was awesome."

124

"Well, it is kinda weird he never mentioned Greg and Raymond to you. I mean, they were your mom's friends. Don't you think it's weird?" He shrugged again. "Maybe he disapproved of them because they're gay."

"What? No. That is so dumb."

"Or maybe there's a side to him that you didn't know about."

What I didn't know was what was happening to my body. It was on fire. And very itchy all over. I could feel my eyes start to burn, and I couldn't even look into Miller's eyes when I told him:

"I open up to you about how it's been super hard since Pop died, and then you literally ruin my summer even more, and tell me he was a complete loser and a jerk. I thought you were my friend. And maybe YOUR Uncle Greg isn't perfect. Ever thought of that? Because you've basically made him sound like a rich snob who hated my Pop."

"Whatever. I know my Uncle's not perfect. But he's a good guy and he's been through a lot. Uncle Greg's had his car windows smashed just for being who he is. And this one time, somebody spray painted swear words on their house in Boston. I know your Pop wouldn't have done anything like that, but he wasn't exactly nice to my Uncles. And sometimes Addie, that's just as bad."

I had stopped listening. I was already walking away. My feet itched, so I just started running toward the lake. What does Miller know about anything?? Pop was literally the ONLY normal person in my family!!

I thought swimming would help...But actually, it made everything worse. I swam so far the lifeguard blew a whistle and I had to turn around. I felt everyone staring at me when I got out. Miller was gone. Not that I was looking for him.

Christy gave me a towel and said, "we're going to get ice cream. Wanna come?"

I wished I hadn't already eaten ice cream with Miller. I wished Miller had never come to the lake.

June 26

Carmen called and asked if I want to go back to Wellfleet for the last week. Maybe she finally felt bad about pawning me off to her worst enemy. Or maybe she needs me to cook mac n' cheese for her while she finishes her proposal. (Mac n' cheese is the only thing I know how to make, but I make it SO WELL, you'd think it's from a five-star restaurant!)

Wouldn't I be happier at Pop's cabin, making mac n' cheese three times a day? You would think so. Because here I'm pretty much a full-time maid anyway. I mean, of course it's my choice to clean. (Yesterday, I agreed to clean up this pile of trash in the backyard. I found Tires, CDs, plastic bags, old kids' toys like a flattened plastic baseball bat and a broken sled. It was like picking up pieces of some other kids' "normal childhood"… HAHA.)

So yeah, you'd think I'd be excited to go back to Wellfleet! It used to be my favorite place on earth, but now it just reminds me of everything I've lost:

I asked Carmen if she'd let me go back to work with Philip at the bookstore, but apparently he has HIRED SOMEONE ELSE! That is SO typical. He WOULD. Just to make me jealous.

And I AM JEALOUS! I'd much rather handle BOOKS all day than clean up people's old crap!

Then Carmen asked me, "Don't you want to come and see how Iris is doing? She's still here with Raymond. He asks about you all the time." Well OF COURSE I want to know how Iris is doing. But she made it sound like she sees Raymond every day and I don't really want to talk to him. I'm sure Miller has already told him what happened at the lake. I tried to change the subject.

"What's gonna happen to all of Pop's stuff in storage?"

Carmen was quiet for a while. Then she blew into the phone. "You know, Ads... I'm just not ready yet. Okay?"

Whatevs. She's coming to get me tomorrow afternoon. I've already packed my stuff. I guess it'll be better to be in Wellfleet... Even though I'll probably just stay locked up in my room.

Steve says I can earn $5 by finishing the backyard cleanup. I probably won't tell Carmen about our little arrangement. She might think it's weird! Haha... But honestly, it was kinda cool of Steve to "hire me." I don't know what else I would've done here! Kyle and I probably exchanged a total of 25 words, and Christy hasn't been back since last weekend. Steve is at work every day... Being here made me realize I didn't really miss anything by not growing up with Steve and Kyle. I mean, I guess it's nice that I was here for a bit. But do I want to ever come back?

And who am I kidding? I'd really like to squeeze that PUG again! So, Right now, feeling O-K-A-Y! Tomorrow, I'll have forty bucks saved up!!

June 27

Scene: "In the Car"
Location: Main highway through Cape Cod
Characters: Carmen & Addie

CARMEN
So. How was it with your dad?

ADDIE
(Shrugs)
Okay, I guess.

CARMEN
(After passing four more exits)
I'm sorry I sent you there... I didn't know what to do.

ADDIE
(Shrugs again)
Whatevs.

CARMEN
Wait a minute. I just apologized, okay.
Shouldn't you apologize to me?
You have no idea what I went through.
I didn't know who else to call—
(Starts crying)

ADDIE
I'm sorry.
But I wasn't running away, you know.
I was just trying to figure stuff out.

CARMEN
Like what? What was so important?
Why didn't you ask for my help?

ADDIE
(Majorly sarcastic)
Really?

CARMEN
Come on. Don't be like that.

ADDIE
Well, it's true.
You pretty much did nothing but
stare at your laptop from
the minute we got to the Cape.

CARMEN
(Huge exhale)
Okay. Yep.
(Very cynical)
It's all my fault. I'm the bad guy
because I have to work. How else
do you think we're gonna make it?
It's not like Pop left me anything.

ADDIE
(Even huger exhale)
This is so dumb.

CARMEN
(After passing two more exits)

It's true. I wasn't gonna tell you.
But he didn't even have a will, Addie.

ADDIE
Well, maybe he wasn't planning to die.

CARMEN
Oh, he knew.

ADDIE
(In shock)
What? Did you?

CARMEN
Maybe.

ADDIE
See??
THAT'S why I had to go looking
for answers on my own.
You tell me NOTHING.

CARMEN
(Getting all worked up)
Okay. What do you want to know?
That he was about to lose the house?
That he had an incurable disease?
That he didn't want us to come here?
Will that make you happy, huh?
To know the real Pop?
Addie, why do you think I haven't
gotten married again?

He was a control freak, Addie.
He liked to pretend there's no such
thing as problems.

ADDIE
(Jaw hanging open)
He didn't want us here? What are you talking about?
You're the one who didn't let me come here!
You're the one who sent me to art camp.
And then you sent my drawings to that school!
I should have been here, fishing with Pop. It was his last
summer!!

CARMEN
(Crying again)
I told him that. Honest. I did.

ADDIE
I don't know what to believe.
You knew he was sick?

CARMEN
He really thought he'd get better.
He was in denial—

ADDIE
How do you know?
How do you know any of this?
Did he tell you?
I don't believe you—

CARMEN
(Swerving off the road all of a sudden)
Okay.

ADDIE
Okay what? Where are you going?
This isn't our exit!

CARMEN
We're going to that storage unit.
I'm gonna let you look through his stuff.
I've been trying to avoid it, so that you could
enjoy your summer. But maybe you're ready.
(Looking at me funny)
You're thirteen, right?

ADDIE
Umm. Yeah.

CARMEN
Okay. I think you're old enough.

ADDIE
(Freaked out)
For what?

CARMEN
You'll see.

Pop's Stuff:

— Tin filled with a small rusted coin collection, some old vinyl records
— Marriage certificate: Charles Kinsley and Rose Cornish, October 9th, 1967
— Birth certificate: Baby Girl Brigitte May Kinsley, born at Plymouth Hospital on February 16th, 1986
— Some photos of baby Brigitte in Wellfleet
—Grandma Rose's drawings and paintings from college (she was really good), Carmen let me take one
—Grandma Rose's death certificate in 1971. (Carmen was only 4 when she lost her mom!)
— Pop's bandannas (I took one)
— Condemned septic form
— New septic tank installed July 2017, invoice for $21,650
— A loan agreement between Charles Kinsley and Greg Sanders, $1,000 per month over 20 months
— Doctor's notice to police, August 9, 2017. Cause of death: complications from recurring aggressive pancreatic cancer, patient refused treatment in final months

June 28 - Back at Pop's cabin.

Except it's not his cabin anymore. Carmen finally told me everything. She said Pop borrowed money against the house (I did not know you can do that?!), and now the cost of it is higher than its value. Like... WHAT? Doesn't she know I SUCK AT MATH?

"It's not worth much, but the payments are still really high," she tried to explain.

"Huh?" (I said it just like that).

"We're losing Pop's cabin. The bank will repossess it soon."

"Oh."

One mystery is solved:

Miller's Uncle Greg paid for the septic tank.

That's where the poop goes!

I'm learning a LOT today. Pop was gonna pay him back over a couple years. So, at least Miller was right about that. But I'm still mad at him.

I told Carmen that Elaine had seen Pop wear a suit. Shockingly, Carmen didn't get mad about me sneaking off to see Elaine. Instead, she said it was probably because Pop went back to Framingham, because his doctor was there. He lived in an apartment and went to work. He was trying to make money, and take care of his cancer.

"I called him last summer," Carmen started, "to see if he could take you while I was in Cambodia. Pop was so stubborn. He thought he could beat the cancer. He thought it would go away. He thought he could fix every problem. He never asked for help. Ever."

I thought about this for a minute.

"That's not true," I said. "Pop asked me to help in the garden. He made me do chores. He had me paint the shed one year."

"That's different. That was him trying to teach you a work ethic."

After that, Carmen and I ate pizza and watched the new Willy Wonka. Johnny Depp is creepy in that movie. I guess that's kind of the point. But it was kinda hard to focus on a movie about a candy factory. Halfway through, I went in my room and cried.

I would give anything to have Pop back. I would ask him so many things.

- Where did you get all those coins in that tin?
- Which of these records was your favorite?
- What was it like when my mom was little?
- What made you buy a house in Wellfleet?
- Were you sad when grandma Rose died?
- Did you really think there was something wrong with Miller's Uncle and Raymond?
- Were you being stubborn about your cancer? Or were you being brave?

Then, I asked myself: What would I do if I was really sick and about to lose my house?

I would probably try to be brave, too.

I would figure something out.

I probably wouldn't ask for help.

Maybe he knew that we wouldn't help him. Carmen doesn't have any money, and she was traveling to Cambodia. Maybe he was feeling the way I always feel — that family is just people you see in June. But the rest of the year, you're on your own.

I'm so tired.

June 29

One good thing:

I've been hanging out with Iris again!! I'm pretty sure Raymond has forgiven me for losing her. I avoided him at first, but then he brought her here... And OMG! I just love this dog so much. She's been snuggling with me on the bed while I doodle. Her little snorts are the best. AHHHH! I could just MELT!

Miller's Uncle Greg is here now! I just heard him come in... I guess he's been out sailing. They all went in the kitchen to talk and it sounds serious... Okay. I'm going into Detective Mode... Iris and I are just gonna "play" in the living room (and eavesdrop).

Greg: "So, Bridge, what are you thinking?"

Carmen: "Well... I guess I'll try to rent it out again."

Greg: "Have you already found someone?"

Carmen: "No... I haven't even listed it yet. I've been slammed with work. What about that Polish lady? You think she'd come back?"

Greg: "I think she's staying in Orleans. She told us it fit her budget better."

Carmen: "Okay... Well, I have to find someone who's willing to pay at least twelve fifty. I have to ask for enough to at least cover half the mortgage."

(Detective Note: I HAD NO IDEA IT COSTS SO MUCH MONEY TO RENT THIS CABIN!)

Greg: "It might be hard to get that much for this house. It's not very big."

Carmen: "Yeah, and then there's the money my dad borrowed from you—"

Greg: "Oh god, Bridge. don't worry about that. Let's just figure out a way for you to keep this place. We'd hate to see you lose it."

Carmen: "The things is, I've been scrambling just to keep up with paying for my house in Maryland. I took on an extra project this month, just so I could pay my own mortgage. So that Addie could spend one last summer here."

(DN: ONE LAST SUMMER? WHAT?!)

Raymond (with British accent): "Tell Brigitte what we've discussed."

Greg: "Well, you can probably guess. We'd like to take it off your hands."

Carmen: "Why would you want to take it on? It's a money pit."

Greg: "Let's just say, I wouldn't be doing it for your dad. He was a piece of work."

All laugh.

(DN: I'm HIGHLY uncomfortable with where this conversation is going. Trying REAL hard to stay in detective mode and act PROFESSIONAL.)

Raymond: "He wasn't all bad. Most of the time. Actually, he never said anything to me. I suppose that's better than finding out what he was actually thinking."

More laughing.

Greg: "Seriously, though, Bridge, if you've thought about selling, we'd like to make an offer."

Carmen: "Seems like a really stupid move, financially."

(DN: It's REALLY hard to stay in detective mode! I DO NOT want someone to own Pop's house who didn't even LIKE HIM!)

Raymond: "And then, you two could have it every summer. Addie could even take care of Iris while we go sailing. Or perhaps not?"

All burst out laughing.

(DN: HAHAHAHAHA! Very funny!)

Carmen: "I don't know what to say... It would mean a lot to us, especially to Addie, to be able to keep coming here. And to see Miller. Those two have been friends since they were babies."

Greg: "Exactly. They need a place to be annoying teenagers. Like us. Remember how we used to get on your dad's nerves?"

Obnoxious laughing.

Raymond: "And then I showed up, and that was really the cherry on top for him, I think. You'd practically have to run away, because your dad didn't let you hang out with us. We really corrupted you, didn't we?"

Carmen: "Remember that stolen bike? Was that me or you? You know, the one from the church parking lot?"

Raymond: "Definitely Greg. No question."

Howling laughter.

Carmen: "No, but seriously, I appreciate your offer to buy the house, but… I just can't take charity from you. From anyone. I've got to figure this out on my own."

Greg: "It's not charity if we're paying what any other buyer would pay."

Raymond: "Besides, what's wrong with a bit of charity? You work for one. Am I right?"

All giggle at British joke.

Carmen: "Why haven't I seen you guys in, like, ten years?" Pause.

Greg: "I wanted my sister to have a chance to bring the kids here. They needed it more than we did. Last summer was our first summer here. It was a total coincidence that I ran into your dad at the wharf that day."

Raymond: "Yeah. A real miracle. He managed to avoid us at all costs."

Laughing again.

Carmen: "How did you get him to accept the money? Dad never took help from anyone."

Greg: "I know. I was surprised too. But he seemed to be really broken up about losing the house. Honestly, I think he did it for Addie. And he insisted it was a loan, that he'd pay us back within a year."

Carmen: "That sounds like him…"

Long silence.

Carmen: "I should've been here. I should've never gone overseas."

Raymond: "Don't be hard on yourself. It's not your fault."

Pause.

Carmen: "Can I be honest with you guys? Since he died, it's been like a weight off my shoulders. I mean, I loved my dad. But sometimes he was just so hard to deal with. And I was never good enough for him, you know? He never told me he was proud of me. Never. Not once."

Raymond: "Well, we're proud of you. I mean, look at the job you've done with Addie. She's got to be one of the most responsible people I've ever come across."

Howling laughter.

(DN: I. AM. S-P-E-E-C-H-L-E-S-S.)

Carmen: "So, you guys really want to buy this house?"

Greg: "We'd love to. And we'd keep Addie's name on the deed."

Pause.

Carmen: "Thank you."

Hugs and cheers.

Raymond: "For Old Man Chuckie. May he rest in peace!"
Glasses clinking.

(DN: literally no words. CASE CLOSED.)

What would Pop think about all of this?!

June 31

We're leaving tomorrow. Carmen's letting me "ride to the bookshop" today. She even gave me a $20 to buy a book for the ride home.

Ha. Yeah right. I'm not going there. I'm so mad at Philip for not paying me and for hiring someone else.
Besides, I'm planning on sleeping the whole way home. My brain is literally MELTING from all the stuff that's happened.

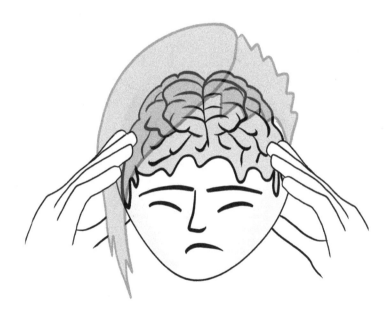

Instead of the bookshop, I'm going to see Elaine.

YUP. I looked at the tide schedule when we stopped at the gas station.

I thought it would help to go talk to Elaine. We're supposed to be leaving REALLY early in the morning, but now I'm not ready to go! It's like I just realized that all this time, I've been here, IN WELLFLEET, which is my favorite place on earth. But it's been like a dream. Not a dream in the good sense either. Like, NOT REAL. Wellfleet isn't Wellfleet without Pop.

I told Elaine how much it hurt to hear Carmen and Greg and Raymond laughing about him. I said I didn't think they deserved to buy his house because of that.

But this is what she said:

"I understand how you're feeling. But I have to say I'm happy you'll be able to keep visiting me."

"But Pop would never sell them the house."

And then I realized what I was saying. I had to ask her. "Greg and Raymond are, you know, married. And Miller claims Pop didn't like them because they're—"

"Gay." Elaine shook her head. "I don't think so. I think Miller's wrong about that. Based on what you told me, I think it had more to do with your mother somehow."

"What do you mean?"

"Well, just think about it. He raised your mother alone, you know? So, maybe he was just... protective of her? That would make more sense to me. Charles Kinsley was a stubborn man. But he was not mean-spirited. He was just trying his best."

148

She handed me a piece of strawberry-rhubarb pie and watched me eat.

(Pop used to watch me eat too. Maybe when you get older, you don't have as many fun things to do? So, like, watching kids eat is super amusing?)

Then she said this: "Either way, I think he'd be happy that you're the one who spends her summers there. And doesn't your friend, Miller, live across the street?"

"Well, I don't know if I'd call him my friend. And now his family is gonna own Pop's house. It's all just too weird."

"Maybe you should sit on it for a while. Let some time go by. Get busy with an art project or something. What else have you got planned this summer?"

"Nothing. Carmen has to go back to Maryland tomorrow. So I'll probably just hang out at my house and wait for my best friend to come back from her vacation."

"Huh. That sounds nice. Is your best friend artistic, like you?"

"Not really. Well, she's a really good singer."

"Is that who you spent last summer with? When you didn't come to Wellfleet?"

"No. Carmen sent me to art camp."

"Art camp?" Elaine basically freaked out. "That sounds amazing! Wouldn't you want to go there this year again? Is it too late?"

I made a disgusted face.

"Oh? It was that bad, huh? A lot of stupid boys or something?"

"No. It's... complicated."

"Well, anything to do with art usually is."

"What do you mean?"

"That's just how it is. They call it an oxymoron. Have you heard that term?"

Elaine continued, "As artists, our greatest need will always be to express ourselves. That's why it's wonderful to see you enjoying it, and that your mother sent you to art camp. Because sometimes, as we get older, it can get harder to continue making art. For some, it becomes impossible. It's often not thought of as a real job. And it certainly doesn't guarantee success. Or even a paycheck."

At first, I thought she was talking about herself, so I asked her, "But don't people buy your metal thingies? I would totally buy one. They're so rad."

"Sometimes, yes. But I'm lucky. I inherited some money, and this property was handed down to me. I'm able to live here and make my art without having to worry. And I never had any children. So, I guess I'm not really talking about myself."

"Who then?"

"Someone I used to know. Someone who used to paint. And then his wife got very sick, and he had to get a real job in the city so he could take care of his daughter. And all of a sudden he realized he hadn't touched his paint brushes in thirty years."

I was watching her face. She was kind of smirking, but, like, almost crying.

"Who are you talking about?"

"A man named Charles Kinsley."

"Pop? Pop used to paint?"

She nodded.

"But my Grandma Rose was the one who... I mean, we just looked at all her paintings in the storage unit. Carmen told me Grandma Rose used to paint in college."

Elaine shook her head. "No. That's not what Charles told me about her."

"He told you about my Grandma?" (WHOA! GOLDMINE! I've N-E-V-E-R heard any stories about her, because she died when Carmen was little, and Pop never talked about her.)

Then Elaine said, "You know it's almost high tide?"

I have NEVER been SO BUMMED about a COASTAL PHENOMENON before

"Listen, Addie. Why don't you call me when you get home to Maryland? We can chat about all this. I have a phone."

"Okay." I was SO not ready to leave.

When I got to the bridge, the water was already covering it. I would have to ride through it, and I knew it was kinda dangerous. I thought about that news article, and about that suit they'd found...And all of a sudden it hit me...

Maybe it WAS Pop's after all. Maybe he threw it into the water. Or maybe he'd been at Elaine's, talking about his paintings, and he'd stayed too long, and had to swim across.

But of course I knew, he hadn't been there all last summer.

But still...

I imagined him swimming along beside me as I rode across the water covered road. Watching over me. Calling out, "Careful, Addie. Keep your eyes straight ahead!"

July 2

I haven't been doodling or writing much. Mindy and I have been at the pool. It's SO fun to be with her again!

But I miss Wellfleet. I miss Elaine, and Pop's house, and IRIS! I even miss the book shop, NOT Philip. But I wish I'd had more time to look around in there.

Most of all, I wish I'd had a chance to get the rest of Pop's art out of storage. I couldn't talk to Carmen about it. Then she'd know I was at Elaine's house instead of the bookshop.

I was lucky just to get back over that bridge...

Anyway. At least I have one of his drawings. It's of his house, or, should I say... Greg and Raymond's house... I'm gonna try to copy it.

Mindy's coming over. We're gonna have a movie marathon.

OMG. Miller sent a message to Mindy's mom.

SO.... YEAH.... Dunno if I'll actually call him. Or go back to Pop's cabin. It might be too weird to stay there, now that it belongs to Miller's uncle. WEIRD.

July 6

We watched the fireworks at the Home Depot parking lot, like always, in the back of the neighbor's truck. Mindy and I had four corndogs each!! I felt SO GROSS.

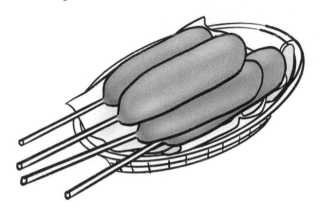

Elaine called yesterday. It's crazy cause Elaine is so old but she, like, never forgets anything.

She said, "When you told me about art camp, you said something about it was complicated. I'd still like to know."

"Oh yeah... well, it has to do with my sketchbook."

"I'm intrigued. I love complicated sketchbook stories."

I sighed into the phone, like, HERE GOES...

I told her the whole story. "Carmen took my drawings from that camp and sent them to an art school. They accepted me, and now I'm supposed to start there next month. But she never asked me if I wanted to go. She just, like, stole my sketchbook and applied without asking me first."

(It actually felt GOOD to tell her! It's weird, but I realized that Elaine's kind of like a grandmother to me...)

Elaine was quiet for an uncomfortably long time before she said, "Hmm. I see."

"And besides. My friend Mindy won't be there. She's like, my ONLY friend. I'm seriously unpopular."

"Hmm."

"Why do you keep saying 'hmm'?"

"I'm just thinking. Well, first of all, I think it's wonderful that your mother wants you to get better at your art. It means she doesn't think it's a waste of time. Secondly, maybe she knows you so well, she had to go you behind your back."

"What do you mean?"

"Well, if she'd asked you about that new school, what would you have said?"

This was a NO BRAINER.

"I would've said NO WAY," I told Elaine. "Carmen knows I HATE change. I mean, that's why she gives me the same exact present for my birthday every year."

"Well, there you go. She knew you'd be too scared to try it. But maybe she doesn't want you to miss out. Ever thought of that?"

"But it still doesn't make it okay."

"Remember what I told you about your grandfather's paintings?"

"Umm... I pretty much haven't thought about anything else since we left the Cape."

"He was just like you, when it came to his art. I actually encouraged him to pick up his paintbrush again." Then, she paused for a while, and I should've guessed, based on, like, EVERYTHING that's happened this summer... that she was about to tell me something IMPORTANT. I held my breath.

"I didn't tell you before, because I thought it might make you sad. But now, I think you need to know."

"Know what?"

"He told me he was sick, Addie."

"What?"

"Yes. That day at the wharf. He told me he was going to Framingham for the summer. He was going to work and to see his doctor. 'To get better,' he said. I invited him over before he left Wellfleet. He agreed."

159

"So… You lied? You told me that was the last time you saw him."

"No. I told you the truth. It WAS the last time. But I rushed home. I made a pie. Then I thought about what else I could do to help him. To send him off with a happy feeling. So, I set an easel out in the yard for him. I even pulled out some of my good oil paints. I wanted to surprise him."

"But he never showed up."

"No. He never showed up."

"I wish you hadn't told me." I was CRUSHED.

"But can you imagine if he'd painted something? Can you IMAGINE?"

I could feel my throat get that horrible tight feeling that comes right before you cry. Before Elaine and I hung up, I thanked her for being such a good friend to Pop. And to me. It's kind of like having a grandma now. I feel like I can call her and talk to her about anything.

Carmen knocked on my door and whispered, "Ads, almost done?" She looked at my face and asked if I was okay.

I cried so hard. She hugged me, and I thought about what Elaine said. That maybe Carmen didn't want me to miss out. Yeah. Elaine is right. I should be grateful that my mom wants me to study art!

What is wrong with me?!

I told Mindy about it. She was like, "Yeah, Ads. You're so lucky. I'm probably gonna end up being a dentist, like my mom, even though all I want is to be a singer."

Thing is, she totally could! Mindy is SUPAH TALENTED! But her mom would never support that dream, it's really unfair.

(I mean, Mindy's version of "Tiny Dancer" is way better than the original. Which is saying a lot because Elton John has been, like, knighted. That's how epic he is.)

July 15

Can't believe how fast I'm getting to the LAST PAGE of this sketchbook!

I don't think it'll last me until the end of summer. Luckily I have enough money for a new sketchbook. I am LOADED. LOL!

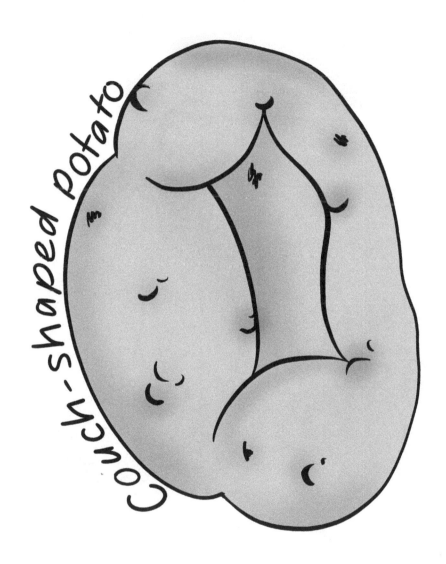

Couch-shaped potato

As you can see, the past week I've been drawing non-stop.

July 18

Something kinda cool happened. But of course, as with EVERYTHING in my life — especially this summer — it started out BAD.

Here's how it went down:

A few days ago, I asked Carmen, "Did you know those paintings were Pop's and not Grandma Rose's?" and she sort of hesitated to say anything. So I was like, "WHOA! You did know, didn't you?" And I was really upset at first, cause, like, why wouldn't she let me have those paintings? And why didn't anyone TALK about the fact that Pop was such an awesome artist?!

So, Carmen finally told me. "Yes, Addie. I've always known they were his."

"Then why'd you pretend Grandma Rose painted them in college?"

"Because... That's the story I always told myself."

Um, what do you mean, STORY? That is SO UNLIKE Carmen!!

So, I'm like, "why?"

"Because, it was just what I needed to do. I'd have rather had a mom who painted. Instead of Pop."

"I don't even know what that means."

"Ads. You have to understand. Growing up with Pop wasn't easy for me. The way he was with you— The way he showed you how to fish? And let you paint the shed? He never did any of that stuff with me when I was growing up. It's like when you came along, he kind of softened up. You changed him. But before that. Forget it. He was not a nice dad."

I was getting mad again. "What does this have to do with the paintings?"

"Well, believe it or not, I got really into painting at one point. I think I was maybe your age, and I REALLY wanted to be an artist and a free spirit. Pop couldn't stand it. He just wanted me to do well in school and stop hanging out with bad people."

"Like Greg and Raymond?"

"What?"

"I heard you guys talking in the kitchen. That night when they told you they wanted to buy the house."

"What did you hear?"

"That Pop ignored them. That he never talked to them."

"Oh, well, I think Pop assumed they were a bad influence on me."

"Poor Pop."

"Yeah. But you gotta understand that pretty much my whole life, Pop had me convinced there was something wrong with me. He was my dad. I believed him when he told me that. And the more he did, the more I hated him. The more trouble I got into."

"What kind of trouble?"

"Well, eventually, I got pregnant with you. But that's not the point. What I wanted you to know is that Pop was very different with you. You didn't know the real him."

"The real him? So, you're saying he faked being nice to me?"

"No. Definitely not." She sighed, like she couldn't really figure out how to tell me something. Then she patted the couch and I sat down next to her. I kinda just wanted her to stop saying mean things about Pop.

But I also wanted her to keep talking about him.

She's NEVER done that with me before!

"Listen. I did want to tell you about Pop's paintings, but I also knew I'd have to explain all this other negative stuff about him to you. It was complicated. So it was easier to tell you they were Grandma Rose's paintings."

"Well, maybe Pop had a reason to stop painting. Maybe he knew that it wasn't a real job. And he had to, like, raise you all by himself, so, he had to get a real job and stop being an artist."

Carmen looked at me for a long time. At first I thought she'd be really mad. But then she said, "Wow. It's actually kind of amazing that you understand that. How are you so smart?"

(HAHAHA! I was just quoting ELAINE!)

"Okay, so you agree, then? Pop did the right thing by taking care of you when you were little, right?"

"Well, yes, but not doing his art also made him bitter."

I shrugged. "I feel like you're bitter too. Sometimes you hate your job."

"Me? No, I don't hate my job. It's stressful and not always fun. But, I'm glad I get to help people. And yeah. I've had to figure out how to keep us afloat."

"So why do you want me to go to art school? Wouldn't it be better if I became a dentist or something?"

"You can be whatever you want. I just want to make sure you don't miss out on doing the thing that makes you happy."

"Like you did."

She hugged me. "I am happy. I'm happy to be your mom."

NOTE: Moms hug their kids all the time. We've just never been like that! But when she hugged me, I sorta realized that Carmen and I are STILL HERE. Pop isn't here...

(And it SUCKS!)

... but Carmen and I are the ones who have to try to keep on living and making sense of everything. I guess a part of me was grateful that we were talking and being better friends.

Then I told her.

"I just feel like everyone's trying to get me to hate Pop. But I really miss him."

"Oh my god, no, Addie. I do not want you to hate him. And there's something you need to understand. Listen to me."

She leaned into the couch and I knew it was gonna be a STORY... (She was finally telling me stuff!)

"At first, when he found out I was pregnant, he didn't talk to me for a long time, okay? I was only nineteen and that was pretty harsh. I had to figure everything out alone. I hated him for not helping me, so I didn't let him see you. But then, after I had you, and you were so cute... I just kept thinking, Pop should meet you. So, I brought you to wellfleet one summer, when you were almost two. And I'll never forget when he first saw you. He totally cried. I'd never seen him cry, okay? It was so sweet. And then, all of a sudden, we were welcome to come here anytime. And so, we just kept coming to visit him. Every summer after that."

when she told me that... I could NOT. STOP. C-R-Y-I-N-G!

"He loved you so much, Addie. It's like, you gave him a reason to keep going. You meant so much to him. You really did."

"Then why didn't we spend last summer with him? Why weren't we there for him when he got sick?"

"That's what I've been trying to explain to you. He loved you, yes. But he was a troubled person. He just carried a lot of anger around. He was stubborn."

"I could've helped him. I could've changed him."

"It wasn't your job. It's never a kid's job to take care of a grownup. Let alone change them."

"But I might have to take care of YOU some day."

"well, yeah. But then you won't be a kid anymore. You'll be a world class artist who makes tons and tons of money with her illustrations. I'll be in some super nice old folk's home. With a hot tub. And a golf course."

I laughed and cried at the same time, which is usually, like, SUPER EMBARRASSING.

But that's what happened...

...if you know what I mean. LOL

Can't believe this sketchbook is almost done!

AND OMG! Guess what?!

This morning, a FedEx truck pulled up in front of the house. There was a huge box FOR ME. It was all of Pop's paintings!!

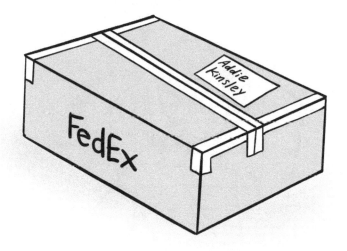

Turns out, Carmen asked Greg and Raymond get them out of storage and send them to me!! I felt weird opening the box in front of Carmen. She helped me carry it into my room, and I've just spent all morning looking at them. Pop was SUCH a good artist! I love ALL OF THEM.

AND GUESS WHAT?!

I found a sketch of ME. I don't know how I missed it before!

Maybe because I thought they were Grandma Rose's, I hadn't really paid attention. But it is SO clearly me. I mean... he got my face pretty much PERFECT. He was REALLY REALLY GOOD!! I can't believe Pop drew a picture of me!! OMG. I am SO happy.

I tried to copy it...Obviously, the original is way better!

I called Carmen into the room. She barged in all flustered like she'd been holding her breath, waiting outside my door.

She saw the drawing and said, "Oh. My. God. Addie! That's you!"

We both stared at it for a long time.

"You must be about five in it. When the heck did he draw this? Oh my god. Remember that little beach chair? And don't you still have that little teddy bear? Looks like you guys were sitting outside, and he got out his pencils and oh my god... I just can't believe this. He actually drew you. He actually drew something."

YEAH!!

So, we're going to JoAnn Fabrics today to have it framed (Carmen has one of those 70% off coupons!) and I'm gonna see what they have for sketchbooks, because THIS ONE IS OFFICIALLY D-O-N-E!! I have NEVER gone through a sketchbook so fast. I guess my life has never been this DRAMATIC before. LOL!

See you in the next sketchbook...

Ps. Maybe Greg and Raymond aren't so bad after all! And I AM kind of excited to see Miller next summer. AND, maybe when they buy the house from us, Carmen will have enough money to buy me an iPhone?

After all, I AM going to a new school, so, like, it would be a REALLY GOOD IDEA...

Cause I will need to text Mindy, like, every 30 seconds

This sketchbook
is officially called

Summer in Wellfleet

because I'm POP's GIRL
FOREVER.!!

BYE!